THE HYENA'S DAUGHTER

THE HYENA'S DAUGHTER

Jupiter Jones

WEATHERGLASS BOOKS

THE HYENA'S DAUGHTER

To a new generation of hyenas – Nancy, Ivy, Arwen and Jessica.

PROLOGUE
1

PART ONE: 1814
5

PART TWO: 1815
68

PART THREE: 1816
125

Francoise Imlay, 1794–1816. Also known as Fanny Godwin.
The first daughter of Mary Wollstonecraft. Her father was the American 'diplomat' Gilbert Imlay.

Mary Godwin, 1797–1851. Better known by her married name, Mary Shelley.
A half-sister to Fanny, born to Mary Wollstonecraft and her new husband, political philosopher William Godwin.

Clara Mary Jane Clairmont, 1798–1879. Mostly went by the name Claire Clairmont.
A stepsister to Fanny and Mary who came into their lives when widower Godwin married his neighbour, Mrs Clairmont.

Prologue

That woman is a hyena in petticoats.
(Horace Walpole)

The End of the Beginning
The Polygon, Somers Town, London, 1797

If she were herself, Mary Wollstonecraft would feel sick as a dog from all the wine they have made her drink. Red wine to compensate for blood loss. But she is not herself. By now, she is half-ghost.

She trails her hand over the counterpane and wonders why the house is so still, so silent, then recollects that it is the small hours, and she wonders if her husband, William Godwin, is asleep downstairs, if her physicians are asleep, and if all those men will be surprised if she lasts beyond daybreak – she notices that they have left the window open a crack to let out her soul, and the night air is cool on her face. She hopes her daughters are asleep. Her Fannikins, and the baby, another girl, nine days old now and taken away to a wet nurse. Even the puppies have been taken away. Puppies they brought for her to suckle, to ease the pain from the contaminated milk that threatened to explode from her breasts, vast and blue and throbbing. Poor puppies, she hopes they thrive, and have good lives, and are loved.

Part One: 1814

After Mary Wollstonecraft's death, her sisters Everina and Eliza write to Godwin, offering to take Fanny. Godwin replies that he intends to parent both his own and the other man's daughter.

Sister, I hear the thunder of new wings.
(*Prometheus Unbound*, P.B. Shelley)

Buttercups

At first, I was Fannikins, and I was everything. Then baby Mary came, and they said my mother was gone. I remember the house stiff with quietness, and for the longest time I was as good as I could be, as quiet as I could be. Quiet when Mr Godwin was thinking, when Mr Godwin was writing, when Mr Godwin had visitors.

Sometimes I was not quiet enough and our maid Marguerite would take me out. I remember her holding my hand as we walked through fields of long wet grass behind the Polygon. And buttercups. Our skirts speckled with wet petals. Holding buttercups to baby Mary's chin to see if she liked butter, and she did.

After a time, Mr Godwin found parenting rather taxing and he looked around for another wife. He married our neighbour, a widow called Mrs Clairmont, and besides a stepmother we didn't really want, we got Claire for a stepsister. She liked butter too.

Three Sisters
Skinner Street, Holborn, London

Our door opens straight onto the world. Straight onto this bursting-at-the-seams city with its bottle shops and chophouses, sinners preaching on corners, fortunes made and reputations lost, a stink of tanneries, a whiff of revolution, and the hurdy-gurdy of narrow streets heaving with hawkers.

Arm in arm and perfectly in step, we three sisters make our way between the people. Orange sellers, slaughtermen in leather aprons, boys running errands, black-hatted Jews, actresses, pickpockets, stevedores, and a man with no eyes who juggles skittles whilst his blue-jacketed monkey goes round with a hat for pennies. We sidestep the flea-bitten monkey and the filth that runs in the gutters. *Goosey, goosey, gander*, we sing as we wander.

We take turns with the basket, with Mrs Godwin's shopping list and the *sing-a-song-of-sixpence* purse. We three are inseparable, invincible, irrepressible. We grin at the gingerbread, cough-syrups and neckerchiefs. Giggle at the hot eels, small coals, pea soup, pickled whelks. Squeal at the pigs' heads, pigs' trotters. *This little piggy went to market.* You're a piggy. No, you're the piggy. You're a piggy-wig-wig.

'Come here, my pretties,' cries a wide woman with a tray of pies and puddings. *Jack Sprat could eat no fat*, we chant and run away laughing.

We pass the place where they hang the men from Newgate prison, hang them like dogs, and we pass a dog pissing in a doorway. We pass a girl, younger than us, selling watercress, and a gin-sodden woman beating her spindle-shanked husband with a stick, and rows of plucked chickens hanging by their scaly yellow feet. We squeeze each other's hands as we skip past the knife grinder who they say has a tail like the Devil tucked into his trousers.

'Ripe! All ripe! See these beauties!' the costermongers cry.

We lose the shopping list, and blind as mice to the consequences, we buy ribbons the colours of *lavender's blue, dilly, dilly, lavender's green*, and a bag of *one-a-penny, two-a-penny, hot cross buns*, and we run home, sticky and laughing.

When we are old enough, we must work. We take it in turns to sit downstairs in the dusty shop, surrounded by books we have already read, to sit in the dimness as the days of our lives tick by. Occasionally the bell on the shop door jangles and someone enters to make enquiries about some volume we don't have, or perhaps comes in by mistake, or to get out of the rain. As their eyes adjust to the badly lit room, they look around at the well-stocked shelves and the empty grate. They do not look at the nothing of a girl behind the counter in fingerless mittens. They do not smile. They do not stay to warm themselves by the fire that has not been lit. They do not disturb the silence, except perhaps for a dry cough politely stifled. Then they inch back out and the shop door clicks shut, leaving us to the shelves of books that we have already read, and to the smell of those already-read books, and the dust, and the cold that creeps under our flannel petticoats, and we sink back behind the counter as the bookish silence closes in once more and the days of our lives tick, tick, tick.

Sometimes we are separated. A flurry of letters and packing. One of us is to be sent away and we don't understand why. Of course, they tell us reasons: one of us is invited to stay with relatives, two left behind at home. One of us is going to school; two stay at home. One of us has eczema and needs sea air; two remain at home. One of us is getting on Mama's nerves; two stay at home.

One sent away will feel special.
Two left behind seethe with resentment.
One sent away will write: how splendid her adventure!
Two write back that they don't miss her.
One sent away feels alone.
Two left at home feel incomplete.
Two left at home fight like she-cats.
One sent away pines for sisters.
Sometimes, if money is not too tight, there is a holiday,

but still, one is left at home. Mr Godwin does not take holidays, and someone must stay to see that he is comfortable.

When our times of the month came, they would be *our* time, not each in turn: her time, and her time, then her time, but always ours, when as one we would be regulated by the moon, as the tides are called to ebb and flow, wolves to howl, lunatics to wander, fish to breed, crabs to moult, water levels in wells to rise, and old wives to pick and plant their bitter herbs, then we would bleed.

By now, we had long been truly sisters, and in the months when one was sent away some drifting might occur, some irregularity, but once back together again we would slip easily into our old pattern, like teeth in a cog, like tumblers in a lock.

We would take chamomile and fennel for the cramps, and we would lie together like spoons, taking turns with a stone flask of hot water wrapped in flannel, taking turns to rub each other's backs, not speaking a word.

Paper Boats
Lynmouth, Devon

Percy Bysshe Shelley crouches by the shoreline, shoes and stockings soaked through. His buff-coloured britches are stained with salt water and his hair whips about his face, with strands getting in his eyes and in his mouth. He is a scribbler of poetry, lanky-limbed, with a laugh like a brandy-sozzled mule and a saucy appetite for sisters. With infinite concentration he creases and folds another pamphlet to make a boat – as he had when he was a boy. You might say he is still a boy, slight and hopeful, boundlessly euphoric, occasionally demonic. He is fully expectant of immortality and impervious to the realities or responsibilities of manhood. Already courting notoriety, he has been sent down from Oxford, tried meddling in politics, tried to establish a Pantisocracy,[1] tried it on with his own sisters (God loves a trier), ditched God and eloped with a girl (and her sister).

---

*1 **Pantisocracy**: A utopic state of communal living dreamt up by poets (male poets, obviously).*

The little boat he makes is as sturdy as paper can be. The words *republic, equality, revolution* all clearly legible. An inflammatory text to be sure. He wishes the little craft a pantheistic godspeed as he sets it upon the ripple of the outgoing tide.

Behind him, amongst the twisted seaweed of the high-water mark, are his ladies, leaning in like bookends. His wife, Harriet, and Eliza, her sister, both slender, pale and quarrelsome. And behind them, the gorse-clad cliffs rise up to the darkening sky.

It is time they left here, time to get gone from this place. It isn't working out as he'd hoped. He and Harriet, perhaps Eliza too, will go to London, to the great metropolis, a world of opportunities, where his more progressive ideas can flourish. He will write again to William Godwin, whose political philosophy he greatly admires. The radical ideas of Godwin's *Enquiry Concerning Political Justice* have ignited a spark, and Shelley is keen to make the acquaintance of the old man. Having recently turned twenty-one, Shelley can now borrow money against his family estate; he will pay a visit to Skinner Street and offer to sponsor Godwin's remarkable work.

As his feet sink into the wet shingle, Shelley folds another pamphlet, struck by how the boat is also a little hat. It would be easy to mistake one for the other.

Maybe a Meteor?
Skinner Street, Holborn

Fanny: We had all read Mr Shelley's letters, and we were all a little in love with him, how could we not love him, with his lofty ethics and words that flew like birds? He was fluent in the glorious idealism of my mother, the radical politics of my stepfather. He was young, rich, soon-to-be-titled. He came blazing into our lives like, like … maybe a meteor?

Yes, he was married. We loved him all the same. Perhaps we loved him all the more. It was safe to love him, for we would love Harriet too.

Mary: Yes, he was married. But marriage – according to my father's philosophy – is an evil and odious monopoly. The worst of all shackles, preventing people from following the dictates of intellect and enquiry. Marriage dooms us to abide our livelong days by the thoughtless and romantic attachments of youth.

Claire: I'm not entirely sure that any of us were following the dictates of intellect and enquiry.

Fanny and the Garden Path
Skinner Street, Holborn

In the garden, Shelley explains his long poem *Queen Mab* to Fanny. Though it is not much of a garden really: you go through the storeroom and through the scullery and through the door that opens onto a yard at the back of the house, and then there is a brick path that leads down a narrow scrap of land with pots of herbs, some gooseberries. Because the path is narrow, two people have to walk quite closely together, even if one of them is married.

When it has rained, as for instance an April shower such as there was earlier this morning when Fanny had to run and fetch in the washing that had only just been pegged out, then the path can be slippery, so that if two people are walking one of them might put an arm around the other's waist, but it would be merely as a helpful precaution, the sort of thing even a married person might do and mean nothing by.

At the end of the garden underneath the elm tree where the starlings roost, there is a bench which is quite big enough for two or even three, but to avoid sitting on the bird droppings, two people might find it necessary to sit closely together, even if one of them is married.

On the bench beneath the elm, Shelley takes his book from the pocket of his jacket, and Fanny notices that the book is folded over, spine creased, pages curled, which is a dreadful way to treat a book, she thinks, and that a person who has his own library really ought to know better.

Shelley reads her some parts of his poem and Fanny sits enraptured. Occasionally, he glances up from his page to notice her brown hair falling over her cheek, her bottom lip jutting, moist. Her hands flicker and clasp in her lap. She pleats a little fold of skirt between her fingers. She feels as if her whole life has unprepared her for this moment. At last she remarks, haltingly, that it is a fine piece. Then, gathering pace, like a snowball barrelling down a steep hillside, she says that she greatly esteems his choice of language, which flows particularly well in the middle cantos, and that the politic of the viewpoint on perfectibility and man's evolution is also especially admirable, and then Shelley says, 'Oh, shut up, Fanny,' and he kisses her on the mouth.

Cusp
Skinner Street, Holborn

Up in the schoolroom, on the fourth floor of Godwin's narrow, gloomy, house and overlooking the garden, not much of a garden, Claire has rolled back a Turkey carpet, somewhat threadbare and in want of a beating. On the floorboards she has chalked a hopscotch grid. At fifteen and a half, almost sixteen, Claire might be too old for hopscotch, but she is often unsupervised and at a loose end. Though she has the curved and creamy-skinned body of a woman, she still has the impulses of a child, and a brattish child at that.

So, with her skirts bunched up in her hands and her tongue sticking out, she hops. When Fanny enters the room, she stops.

'I saw you,' Claire says. 'What were you talking about?'

'I thought you had French lessons this afternoon?'

'Monsieur Gérard left. He says he hasn't been paid since Christmas. He says we are all *mendiants et voleurs*.' Claire rolls her eyes and extravagantly acts the part of the aggrieved Frenchman. Then she asks, 'Fanny, are we poor?'

'Goodness, no! Not poor, not really poor, just that everything, indeed yes, *everything* is on credit, which is perfectly normal, but with credit it can be a matter of timing, which has been all wrong lately.' Fanny spies a scatter of mouse droppings along the wainscoting and wonders what Mrs Godwin's cats did all day. They didn't earn their keep, that was for certain.

'I saw you,' Claire says again. 'I saw you and Mr Shelley sitting under the tree, and I saw—'

'Oh, shut up, Claire,' says Fanny.

Pox
Skinner Street, Holborn

Not that the marks sadden her particularly, but Fanny is aware that close to, the eye may see, fingers may read, the small round marks in her skin. Shelley called them the fingerprints of angels, and later, on reflection, Fanny will wish that she had blushed. How pretty that would have been, the rose flush of her skin under his fingertips. But no. That's not how it happens. As Shelley lightly, tenderly touches those small, pale scars on her face, Fanny feels the colour drain from her like water from a sink. White, clammy, stammering, she tells him of Mr Haygarth's methods for the cure and prevention of smallpox;[2] of how her resourceful, clever mother knew of the methods; how in Le Havre in the midst of an epidemic she had bathed her Fannikins and kept her skin cool. Faltering slightly, Fanny prattles on about how by education and cleanliness

---

2 **Smallpox:** *Endemic in Europe since the time of the Crusades, smallpox was often fatal. Those who pulled through were sometimes badly scarred, and Fanny's pocked complexion was unfortunate but far from unusual.*

many more lives might be saved, and Shelley inches away as if he fancies himself contaminated, though Fanny has not been contagious for almost twenty years.

Smitten
Skinner Street, Holborn

If there is one thing Godwin despises, it's cats. He trips over the black one in the passageway from his study, and in the parlour he mistakes the tortoiseshell for a cushion. The white one, the one that sheds hairs, sits on his wife's lap and eyes him with something like pity.

'I have just now written to the Wollstonecraft Aunts, Eliza and Everina, in Dublin,' he says. 'To ask if they might take Fanny.'

Mrs Godwin purses her lips, says nothing. There is no need. Then she says, 'Fanny's a weak little ninny to have her head turned so. And him a married man.'

'And if not Dublin, perhaps Fanny might go to Aunt Lydia in Wales until this blows over,' Godwin says.

'Blows over?' his wife screeches, dislodging the white cat. 'For all his fancy waistcoats and progressive ideas, that young man of yours is a disaster walking. A disaster. You should never have encouraged him, Godwin, however much he flattered you, however many post-obit notes he proffered.[3] If he ruins Fanny – silly girl that she is – he ruins all three.' Here, she wags her finger at him. 'You know how it will look for my Claire, and for Mary too. If Fanny is embroiled in some *ménage à trois* scandal, Lord knows the damage will not stop at *trois*.'

'You know best, my dear,' says Godwin, surreptitiously aiming a kick at the white cat now looking for somewhere to sharpen its claws. But the cat merely arches its back and inscribes its mark on the sofa leg. Godwin pretends not to notice. Noticing, in the domestic sphere, is something best left to Mrs Godwin.

'What does Mr Shelley see in poor Fanny? That's what I'd like to know,' his wife continues, loud and unabated. 'She's a mouse. Hardly a great beauty, or a wit, with no fine prospects.' Mrs Godwin has no cares about being overheard.

'She has fine intellectual capital,' says Godwin, reasonably, in Fanny's defence. He means on her Wollstonecraft side by nature, and by nurture from his parenting. And besides, he is fond of her.

'Intellect!' snorts his wife. 'Is that what the young man's after? The lecherous cock-a-doodle-dandy that he is.'

---

3 **Post-Obit:** *A type of bond where an amount of money is borrowed at a steep rate of interest, on the promise that a considerably larger amount will become repayable on the death of a person from whom the borrower is to inherit funds. In Shelley's case, he expected to inherit an unentailed part of the family estate from his elderly grandfather, Sir Bysshe Shelley of Castle Goring in Sussex. For the lender, there was always the risk of the old bugger outliving the borrower.*

Fanny Longs for News from Home, but Today Is Sunday
Pentredevy, Carmarthenshire

'Your mother,' says Aunt Lydia to Fanny, 'she was a one. All that book learning, it did fill her head with so much nonsense, she didn't know her place.'

Lydia, old before her time, stoop-backed, black-frocked, papery skinned and liver-spotted, is not Fanny's aunt but the second wife of her maternal grandfather. Still, family of sorts, and it is good of her to take Fanny in, and at such short notice.

'*Ydych chi'n barod, Modryb?*' asks cousin Gwilym, who is not Fanny's cousin but the widowed brother-in-law of Lydia's youngest sister, so family of sorts. Short-legged and fusty-smelling, Gwilym doesn't live at Lydia's but arrives early each day and makes himself at home.

'*Rhaid i ni beidio bod yn hwyr,*' Lydia says, tying the strings of her bonnet as if she were about to step out into a force-ten gale. '*Ond merch araf, ddiofal yw hon. A di-dduw hefyd.*'

Fanny picks out the one word: *araf*, which she has learnt

means slow, and she guesses they are talking about her because they both look. Gwilym's look strips her naked, Lydia's hands her a blanket.

'Rush you now, Fanny. We mustn't be late for Chapel.' Lydia is animated by the fear of God, and her God is a hellfire-and-damnation patriarch, an all-seeing final arbiter with keys to the gates of Heaven chained to His almighty belt, and Chapel is twice on Sundays.

Fanny offers Aunt Lydia her arm as they walk. Lydia refuses; she has Gwilym's.

'Did you perhaps keep any letters from my mother that I might read?' Fanny asks.

'*Duw, duw.* No, child. What there was, we lit the fire with.'

The Grave of Enlightenment; the Spark of Romanticism
St Pancras Churchyard

Mary pretends to understand why Shelley says he expects to die soon. Obviously, everyone knows they are going to die. But soon? They lean against her mother's modest mausoleum, side by side, her head resting on his shoulder, and they watch a beetle climb up a stalk of grass. Not a fancy beetle, iridescent and scintillating, or a stag beetle with horns. Just an ordinary workaday beetle, blackish and small, going about its business. It reminds Mary of Fanny, and she stifles a snort of laughter; Shelley has a great affection for Fanny and dislikes her being made fun of. The beetle reaches the end of the stalk, forelegs waving into nothingness. The stalk leads nowhere. Will it leap or retreat?

No point in living past thirty, he says. Becoming an old man, resting on past glories like Godwin, whingeing about money and reputations.

The stone behind them is warmed by the sun, the ground is slightly damp; an invisible process going on all around.

When she was travelling in Sweden, Mary wonders, did her mother ever meet Wallerius? Discuss with him his theory of evaporation? So clever, so obvious. Mary, this Mary, wishes she could ask her mother not about evaporation but about this scheme of Shelley's. About travelling to the Alps.

Before he dies, he must live, he says. Be free. Breathe the air, he says.

The beetle is still perplexed. Perhaps. Or perhaps it is wrong to attribute such consciousness to an insect. Shelley waits for her answer. The stone at her back offers no advice. Mary shifts slightly, shifts the angle of her head. Shelley strokes her hair.

Presently, Shelley flicks the beetle away over the short-cropped grass between the graves, and Mary begins to plan which books she will take with her.

Gylfinirod, Crëyr a Gwylan[4]
Pentredevy, Carmarthenshire

There are only three books in Aunt Lydia's house. One is a book of sermons, a monolithic slab, black-bound, locked shut. Its key is kept in the best teapot. The second is an indecipherable spider-written notebook of recipes and remedies that lives on a high shelf next to the teapot. Fanny finds the third quite by accident and can only think that some previous guest might have mislaid it, left it behind in the musty storage space under an upstairs window seat. Mr Bewick's *A History of British Birds*, volume two; to Fanny's delight, it is in English, with some translations into Welsh pencilled into the margins. On one of the afternoons when there is a pause in the slanty rain, she walks down to the estuary.

Identification is harder than she expected. Some of the waterbirds are white; a type of gull she thinks. Gwylan, perhaps, and she says the word silently to herself. But many are medium-sized and modestly speckled brown and grey and

---

4 **Gylfinirod:** *Welsh for curlew. A wading bird with a mournful cry.* **Crëyr:** *heron.* **Gwylan:** *gull.*

others are speckled grey and brown. Fanny watches, trying to pick out their individual characteristics, the way they move. Some stab with long, sharp beaks. Some have bills like spoons; they push their faces into the silt as if they are ashamed of something. Some of the birds have bright red legs becoming spoiled with knee-high mud stockings. Some of the birds notice her; most do not.

Fanny picks her way along the waterline. Watching the birds, she is hardly aware of the stealthy, briny swell seeping through the salt marsh – an intricate tufted maze of shifting loyalties where land becomes sea and sea becomes land. Ahead, she hears the cries of all the birds she hasn't learnt the names of yet, curlews, egrets, redshanks and plovers, and she has the strangest feeling of being adrift, of this moment, *this* moment being fleeting, never to be repeated. She can never again be here and now at this point in time before anything too terrible has happened.

She slips and slithers across the wet ground, stumbles over reedy tussocks and through ribbony rivulets that squelch under each step. If she could only round the point that juts out into the flatness she might get out of the mud and reach a place where the shingle is more wholesome underfoot. She might search for pebbles, find a perfectly smooth one to keep in her pocket. A pebble to remind her of this strange place and this moment and how she feels, to remind her of the haunting, spiralling call of the birds out in their vast, empty-looking landscape. But it is further than she thinks and she will have to turn back. She should have started out sooner.

Before It Was Light
Skinner Street, Holborn

Inky black and heavy as shame, the darkness lies across Claire's chest. She thinks of birds, fragile, impossible birds still sleeping in trees with their heads under their wings. The ones with the biggest eyes will wake first, blackbirds and robins. Then the pretty finches. The skylark poet told her so. Told her while he traced feathers on the inside of her wrist. But for now, the sky is quiet.

Treacle black and ordinary as blankets, the darkness is pushed to one side as Claire rises from her warm nest. She thinks of Mama sleeping on her back with her mouth open, dreaming of revenge; of Mr Godwin lying next to her, dreaming of his first wife. She laughs silently at the thought of their fury when they discover two of their girls have flown.

Truffle black and risky as lips, the darkness caresses her legs as she pulls on her stockings and fastens them with blue ribbons. Her petticoats and dress are ready, her bag packed. *Tout sont prêt.*

Claire goes on tiptoes to the window and inches back the thick curtains, careful of the clatter of brass rings along the pole. She hears now the solemn flap of an owl, sees the faintest wash of grey to the east. The poet said he would be waiting for them at the end of the street. She holds her breath listening for hooves or the creak of a carriage wheel, but there is nothing yet; *il n'y a encore rien.*

A muffled tap-tap on the door, and her stepsister Mary slides in with a rustle of her best brown silk and the faint smell of violets.

'Mary, you're dressed already. Help me with my stays. *S'il vous plaît,*' Claire says.

The French is important; it is her passport, her ticket, her *billet.* Mary hasn't had lessons like Claire has, Mary, reluctantly, has agreed to Claire going with them because the poet says they will need Claire to translate. Once they reach the French coast, Claire will be invaluable, he says.

Mary pulls and Claire breathes in, and in, sucking her thoughts into a tight knot under her ribs. The poet loved Fanny first and Fanny loved him back, but diffidently. Now he loves Mary, and she loves him back devotedly. Finally, he will love Claire, she is sure of it, and she already loves him back. Loves him —? She searches for an adverb. Despite the French lessons, she is not as clever as her sisters, but she will love him – extravagantly, secretly, slavishly. Darkly.

Scandal!
Turnagain Lane, Holborn

Have you heard?

What's that, my lover? asks the woman with the basket of eels.

The chair mender's wife raises her voice, exaggerates her lip movements and says it all over again. She doesn't mind repeating herself.

That man on Skinner Street, the book man with the long nose. He's only gone and sold his daughters!

Never! All three?

No, not all of them. Apparently the gentleman would only take the two pretty ones, the fair and the dark. Fifteen hundred guineas the pair, so I heard.

Thomas Jefferson Hogg Is Quizzed
Bournemouth, 1853

Q: Mr Hogg, you and Percy Bysshe Shelley were at Oxford together, but do you remember the first time you met Mary Shelley?

TJH: Oh yes, we had a high old time. Got sent down in the end. Nonsense about that pamphlet.

Q: And Mary Shelley?

TJH: Of course. I'm getting fat. Gouty and a bit deaf these days, but I still remember it exactly after all this time. Strange as a thunderclap.

Q: Strange? Do go on.

TJH: Well, I thought Shelley was soft on the other one, the older sister, because the two of them used to sit together thick as thieves discussing poetry and politics and the Devil knows what. A bit too intellectual for my tastes, but Miss Fanny was Wollstonecraft's daughter, d'you see? She was pedigree in Shelley's book.

Q: I didn't know that. But Mary Shelley, when did you meet her?

TJH: Ah, that. Well, we called at Godwin's one day and were loitering in the shop. We did a lot of loitering back then, Shelley and me. Masters of loitering and lurking. And I assumed that Shelley had planned another assignation with Miss Fanny, when blow me, this other sprite sprints across my field of vision. Not a woman, a girl, with pale bright hair and an outlandish frock, like the get-up they go in for north of the border, and the silk was the swishiest silk, and she pipes up, 'Shelley?' And he says, 'Mary!', and that was that, d'you see?

Q: So it was love at first sight?

TJH: Always was a sly old dog. Well, no, not old, Shelley was never old. A boy really. But damn me, the brass neck of him, cheating on the divine Harriet with not one but two of Godwin's girls.

Fanny Is Recalled from Wales
Skinner Street, Holborn

The day-long jolting coach from Bristol has left Fanny bone-weary, fretful from cramped inactivity and the anticipation of uproar. The house is not in uproar. In the thirteen days since Mary and Claire's dawn flit with Shelley the house has passed through stages of shock, outrage, desperation, and has settled into torpor and a brooding ineffectiveness.

Fanny lets herself in, takes off her coat, and because yet another maid has left without giving notice, she makes her own tea and carries a cup through to Mrs Godwin, sulking in the parlour, and one to Godwin, sulking in his study.

She hovers, asks gentle questions, tries to avoid treading where she shouldn't. She pieces together the events and the non-events that have occurred in her absence. She learns, bit by bit, that whatever could be done to recover the silly girls has been done. Mrs Godwin had packed a bag and instantly followed the silly girls to Calais, followed them like a bloodhound, determined, at the very least, to recover her own Claire, obviously the victim of abduction or coercion, but Claire had inexplicably refused to return home with her mother.

'Mrs Godwin was not persuasive enough,' says Godwin, barely looking up from his papers. 'She thinks she is a force to be reckoned with, that her words carry weight …'

Godwin had apparently remained at home, despairing about the silly girls and writing letters. 'A Waste Of Space,' says Mrs Godwin, inflecting every word with a capital. 'The great and wise philosophist Mr Godwin is a waste of space. "I will send a letter," he says. A letter! A letter! He should save his ink to cool his porridge. As if a letter would make those silly girls understand that this world does not revolve around poetry and some goose-brained, grandiose idea of so-called "free love", but around three meals a day, around property and income and reputations. Oh, sometimes I despair of Godwin and his pointless waste of ink.'

While Mrs Godwin huffs and flaps her hands to cool her flushed cheeks, Fanny retreats to the kitchen.

Oh, those silly adventurous girls. Fanny can see that Mrs Godwin is right, of course she is right. Claire is now lost by association, lost to the utmost disgrace, and it is only natural and maternal that Mrs Godwin should blame Mary. Mary, a feckless minx with no sense of shame, according to Mrs G. And you know who she gets that from. And yes, Fanny does know. But Mary is her sister and dearer to her than life itself and it is hard to be angry with her. Fanny bites her lip. Poor Mary. Mary is in love and so already, so very, very lost.

Holding the small, bone-handled knife, Fanny reflects

that she had lately fancied herself to be in love, and yet here she is, where she is needed, standing at the sink, peeling slightly shrivelled onions to make soup because no one has eaten.

She cuts off the root ends, pares away the brown papery layers; her eyes begin to brim. But it's just the onions. On the inside, under her apron, her dress, her stays, chemise, her skin, and inside her ribs and intercostal muscles – a lattice to hold and contain – is the pericardium, a purse that holds the heart. And though her heart is raw with grief, no one cries about it.

How to Be Angry
Skinner Street, Holborn

— Think about how she killed your mother. Indirectly.

— Know that she has the stronger claim on ~~your father~~ the only father you have ever loved. That she is careless of his love and his favouritism. That she says horrible things about him (only some of which are true).

— Consider, <u>for almost certain</u>, that the poet loved you first. Dwell on this.

— But Mary gets what Mary wants. Mary wants her own way. You are ~~inconsequent~~ unimportant in Mary's scheme of things, brushed aside, easily forgotten. Brood on this.

— Remember that she was always a crybaby. That you always made excuses for her, held her hand, took the blame even when she pulled your hair, called you poxy. Remember that time she smashed your cup, the one Mr Godwin gave you, the one with an *F* on it, the one you had had since before she was born, the one you had when you were Fannikins. And that when *you* cried, she laughed at you, and said it was only a stupid cup and you were stupid to be so sentimental. And that just when you really did hate her, she ran to the garden to fetch you a strawberry, and you had to forgive her, ~~although the strawberry was quite a small one and you could see that her lips were stained with juice~~.

— And she hasn't changed. When Mary thinks no one is looking, she cheats at cards, but you are *always* looking, and you say nothing, and anyway, sometimes you lose on purpose.

— Reflect that the poet loved you, for almost certain, he loved you first. Now wrap up this stupid idea and put it away, it is nothing. *You are nothing.*

— Remember that she killed your mother. Indirectly. That she is your mother's daughter. That by leaving you, she orphans you all over again.

But it is hard to be angry with a sister. Hard to be angry with a sister when you are all that is left of each other's mother. Hard to be angry when you *are* each other's mother, and without her, you are nothing.

Back
Gravesend, and various other parts of London

Then, just as abruptly as they had left, those silly, adventurous girls came back. On arrival, hungry and dog-tired, Mary and Claire must traipse about after Shelley, knocking on doors, trying to raise enough money to pay off their passage – sailing back along the Rhine and then across the North Sea from Rotterdam. Shelley had promised the boat's captain he could easily supply the funds once they got to London. The captain scratched his beard and nodded. The young gentleman and his two companions looked well heeled and spoke the way of well-bred sorts, but a debt is a debt, and even toffs have been known to spring a rig. So when they dock at Gravesend, the captain sends one of his men to chaperone them until the debt is discharged. The boatman he sends, Joshua Bone, is tired. He has three days' shore leave due and is anxious to get back to his wife, who is in labour. Please, God, let this one be a son; he has five daughters already. The young gentleman rings the bell of another door, of another house, of another friend, who he says will certainly be in a position to lend some money. Bone is a quiet man. Bone closes his eyes and quietly sighs when the gentleman says they must try another address. When the gentleman runs out of friends, he declares that as a last resort they must apply to his wife for the money. Bone raises his eyebrows and glances again at the two young ladies and prays hard for his baby to be a boy.

Cuckoo
Skinner Street, Holborn

Fanny lies awake in the springtime night, clammy and so very wide awake. She hears the near and the distant church bells chime the small hours. Stepney, Bow, St Clements, all the bells of the old rhyme. *You owe me five farthings. When will you pay me?* And *here comes a candle to light you to bed*, but hers has guttered out long since and the darkness is a shell that encases her. She drifts into a dream where she locks hands with Mary. Fingers interlaced, they make an archway. Claire, skipping, laughing, dips below the guillotine of their outstretched arms. And her father, her real father, prowls through Paris with his collar turned up and—

Somewhere in the restless dark, a chime of three, then the quarter, then the half hour. Sparrows and starlings roosting in the eaves pay no heed to the bells.

Before the dawn, Fanny dreams she hatches from an egg. She comes out wet and hungry. She must fledge and learn to fly. Her skin prickles as feathers begin to erupt, downy feathers, ugly feathers, grey, useless, flightless feathers. Another bell chimes, *I do not know*, and in the silence behind its reverberation another egg hatches, an egg that Fanny hadn't seen because her lids are gummed shut over half-formed eyes. The new hatchling barrels her out of the nest and she is falling, falling, falling. She lands hard, and when she wakes, she is cold and next to naked on the garden path, and—

The Lock of Hair
Skinner Street, Holborn

Folded in the paper is a lock of Mary's hair – she has little else to give – and Fanny cautiously opens the small packet and stares at the loop of pale brown, not-quite-blonde hair, tied with a narrow lavender-blue ribbon. Her sister's hair has always been fine and pale, finer than her own, paler than her own. More golden and inclined to gleam in the light, inclined to catch the eye of a fickle-hearted young poet.

'What have you there?' asks Mrs Godwin, not looking up.

'Nothing,' says Fanny, pushing the problem to the bottom of her sewing basket.

Mrs Godwin's indifference falls away at that one word. 'Nothing' almost always means something. 'Show me,' she demands. And, jumping to conclusions, she declares, 'It's a letter! It's a letter from my Claire, or from' – and she pauses – 'from *her*.'

From Mary.

Mary, Claire and Shelley are back in London, but

Godwin, mindful of the gossip and fearing damage to his own reputation, will not have the girls back at Skinner Street. Fanny shrinks herself into her thin, brittle shell and squints carefully as she threads a needle.

Mrs Godwin continues with her quizzing: 'Or is it from —?'

Mr Shelley's name can hardly now be mentioned, not since he captured her own innocent girl, captivated Godwin's shameless girl, and now all three are living, brassy as you like, in seedy lodgings somewhere.

'Show me.'

Slyly, Fanny tries to slide the lock of hair out of the fold and into her threads, but Mrs Godwin springs like a cat across the hearthrug and grabs Fanny's wrist, twisting and pinching until she has what she wants, and then, when she sees what it is, there is pandemonium. How dare Mary write, how dare she send such a token of sisterly affection, how dare Fanny accept the packet, knowing the hand, knowing exactly who it was from, then attempt to conceal it. Such ingratitude. Such treachery. How dare Fanny betray Mr Godwin's household by flagrant fraternisation. She shrieks for Mr Godwin, who hears but doesn't come.

At that very moment, Mr Godwin is in his study writing to the very same Mr Shelley, petitioning for desperately needed funds of fifteen hundred pounds, the theft of his girls notwithstanding. Mrs Godwin is sure she does not know how her husband can hold two such contrary points of view simultaneously. Really she hasn't the head for such confusing multiplicity, so she deals with just this one thing and sends Fanny to her room.

Like a child, Fanny bears the tirade of accusations and abuse. But she is a grown woman, and her heart heaves and breaks all over again for the blatant hypocrisy of a stepfather, the loss of a poet, the loss of her sisters, the loss of a lock of fine, pale hair.

Worm
Church Terrace, Pancras

When the money ran out and Mary and Claire and Shelley came home, just as the boat was docking at Gravesend it heaved to one side, and Mary thinks that in that moment, she must have accidentally swallowed Claire. Now, in Mary's gut, Claire grows; she feeds on her host, and her length increases, while Mary is pale and thin.

The Microscope
Church Terrace, Pancras

Shelley announces that he and Claire will walk. Contrary to the show of ease put on for all the world, they are now so poor that they cannot afford a carriage from their lodgings in Pancras to Holborn, where he will sell his microscope. Before they go, Shelley and Claire breakfast on tea and a little bread. Claire would have liked some butter, but Shelley has given it up and will not have it in the house.

'We should get ten pounds at least. After all, it's a fine specimen,' says Shelley, speaking not particularly to Claire, just that way that he does, in dialogue with himself, which ought to be a monologue but apparently isn't. 'Perhaps twenty. Yes, twenty pounds, a very fair price for the old flea glass.'

If they secure twenty pounds, wonders Claire, might they have dinner? A ride home? Shelley owes money and is dodging bailiffs, but he will probably spend the proceeds on more books. Claire longs for cake. She is still hungry, and it is making her tetchy. She would, she thinks, eat the entire grisly contents of Mr Hooke's *Micrographia*, preferably boiled until soft and palatable, in a pudding with suet – another thing Shelley eschews. Hmmm, louse pudding? Yes please.

She pitter-pats after Shelley's long, loping stride to visit Mr Harris, an optician who keeps shop in a filthy ginnel, the worst part of Holborn, and Claire thinks, poor man, he must have more need of the twenty pounds than they ever do. Yet when shown into his private rooms, she notices that beneath his shop jacket of plain stuff is a waistcoat of handsome black brocade with buttons of mother-of-pearl, tiny buttons, she has never seen finer. The waistcoat is not showy or ostentatious but will have cost a pretty packet, of that she is sure.

Mr Harris takes the magnification machine, examines the brass, the knurling, the lenses. Shelley rocks on his heels and runs his fingers through his hair. Claire fixates on the neatness of the tiny stitching of Mr Harris's buttonholes. She hopes the bailiffs have not yet found out their address, for sharp-eyed Harris sees only scratches, water damage and inferior workmanship. He offers a niggardly five pounds for the microscope. Shelley snorts, packs it away in its velvet-lined travelling case, and the two men bow and part on civil terms.

'There's always Mr Davidson's on Skinner Street,' says Claire.

'Davidson's it is then, I suppose,' returns Shelley rather flouncingly.

They traipse to Skinner Street, avoiding number 41 as they are still very much *persona non grata* with Godwin and Claire is anxious to avoid the embarrassment of her mother. They approach stealthily from downwind, slip inside Davidson's emporium, and after some tooth-sucking and posturing, Shelley accepts an offer of five pounds.

They return home triumphantly to Pancras with four pounds, eighteen shillings and fruit cake to find that Skinner Street, in the form of a note from Fanny, has come in their absence. Dear anxious thoughtful Fan has risked the wrath of Mrs Godwin to warn that bailiffs have found out their address and they must move again.

Puss

You remember when you were Fannikins. You remember the maid, Marguerite, crying. She had her hands over her face, and the noise and the wetness was seeping out between her fingers. It was the first time you'd ever seen a grown person weep; you were surprised to learn that they did. And you laughed.

Back then, when you were Fannikins, you had Puss instead of sisters. But one day Puss lashed out, a mad thing, hissing, spitting. She tiger-striped the back of your mother's hand with her claws, then, with all her fur standing on end, she yowled and dashed up the chimney.

You didn't cry when they took Puss away in a sack to be drowned. Marguerite cried, and then you cried when you were spanked for laughing.

An Economy
Skinner Street, Holborn

Samuel Johnson's *Dictionary of the English Language*, first published in 1755, includes an entry on ladies' undergarments: 'Stays (n. without singular): Boddice; a kind of stiff waistcoat made of whalebone, worn by ladies.'

The stays of particular interest to Fanny – belonging once upon a time to her mother Mary Wollstonecraft and marked with her initials to save them from getting lost in the laundry – have been carefully stored all these years in an old trunk. Moths have got in and had their way with some of the other garments but have declined the stays. The stays are not of course wholly made of whalebone, like a carapace, an exoskeleton for the ladies to don like armour, but instead they are made of stiffened fabric with narrow strips of bone stitched into them and tightened about the wearer's body by means of criss-cross lacing. Had the second Mrs Godwin not been so broad in the beam she would no doubt have had them for herself, but as they didn't suit, Fanny might have the use.

Laced into the stays, did Fanny feel encircled by motherlove?

Did she feel constricted by the expectations of 'such a mother'?

Did she feel diminished by the economy of hand-me-downs?

Were the stays a spur, a vindication of rights?

Did she wear them as a badge of honour?

A hair shirt?

A comforter?

Or, after all, a carapace?

Drowning in Debt
Nelson Square, Blackfriars

Letters now pass frequently between the Godwin and the Shelley households, sometimes via the post, sometimes by hand, thus saving the 4d postage. Fanny traipses back and forth, bearing their senses of entitlement and of injustice, their polite formalities, their requests, recriminations, hypocrisy, animosity, grudges, suspicions and petty resentments like so many fleas in her ear.

With a letter from Godwin to Shelley in her pocket, she knocks on the door of the house just off Blackfriars Road.

'They pulled another woman from the river,' says Claire by way of greeting.

Fanny looks startled. 'Alive?' she asks, but she's thinking dead. Dead and cold. And wet, obviously, with her skirts billowing around her head in the water. Then dragged out, hauled onto the bank, or into a boat, by men, always men, rescuers with a sense of importance and a chance of playing the hero, or a chance of reward. You never knew. Not for sure.

'Alive,' says Claire. 'Apparently.' She holds open the door and Fanny squeezes past into the latest of a series of lodgings. This, like the others before it, is precarious, cramped, untidy.

'Somewhere over towards Limehouse, and she was reanimated by a surgeon,' says Claire, revelling in the melodrama of it.

Fanny pauses, searches around for a memory she might have lost — something that happened when she was small. The event is a matter of record. It's in her mother's journal, in her private letters to Fanny's father, and as Godwin's love had known no shame, it is published for all the world to know in the *Memoirs*. The scandalous *Memoirs*, which had so displeased her Aunts because of the tarnish to the family name and to their school.

But knowing in that way is not at all the same as memory. Fanny closes her eyes as if the darkness might help. She feels in her pocket. She knows what happened: that her mother, feeling utterly rejected, had jumped off Putney Bridge to drown, was rescued and had to carry on living. But that is just fact, it has no body or weight, you cannot cradle it like a pebble in the palm of your hand. Does she remember? Or does she only remember being told, or more probably, quite pointedly, *not* told where her mother had been, why she had been gone so long, why she had come home with her hair unpinned, dirty, still damp.

'Take your coat off, Fan, if you are staying. Mary should be down in a moment.'

'And Shelley?'

'Another flit. Bailiffs again. He'll be back on Sunday.'[5]

Fanny wonders why on earth Shelley keeps promising to lend Godwin money when he has nothing but debts himself and must lie low for six days of the week. She lays her coat over the arm of a chair and sits stiffly beside it. Claire lolls on the other side of the hearth, devouring the dense newsprint, the details of the rescue, and the dead woman revitalised.

---

5 **Bailiff:** *Bailiffs were only able to execute writs and seize goods from Monday to Saturday. They had no authority at all on Sundays.*

A Little Spark May Yet Remain
Putney Bridge, 1795

Samuel Pettiman and Johnny Knuckles are eel men: a little night fishing and a lucrative sideline in keeping an eye out for those who slip into the river by mistake. It's easily done, an ill-judged manoeuvre betwixt gunwale and jetty, a too-hasty tread on a slick, beslimed step. Despite the risks, few bother learning to swim. And then there are those who mean to slip out of this world. This one was a quiet one, hardly a splash.

'Take her legs, Johnny. Take 'em, she won't bite. Lord, but she's a lump.' Heavy with the weight of water, they get her, somehow, into the skiff and scull upstream. Johnny takes off his coat.

As soon as the object is got out of the water, it should be wrapped in a greatcoat and conveyed to the nearest receiving house ...

Fortunately, the Swan with Two Necks is not far. Not far at all. There, they have a box from The Society with instructions, equipment and an address to apply to for the payment. They have what is necessary to sustain the living and to bring back the dead.

'Hey! Hey! Mr Melville, we 'ave one. No lady by the looks, but the reward's the same.'

Just the same, though not as liberal as what it was. 'Bring her in, boys! Not in there – take her through to the kitchen. Lady or not, she don't need no gawpers.'

The body is to be laid near the fire, and as pure air is essential to the return to life, not more than six persons are to be present ...

They manhandle her onto a scrubbed deal table and out of her clothes. Drizzle her with brandy, rub her with flannels. Melville stokes the fire to get a good blaze, and while his back is turned, Johnny swigs the brandy and chokes. The woman is a cold stone. She is leaving behind a daughter, Fanny, a work of as yet unrecognised literary genius, and the cold shoulder of a feckless adventurer. She believes she has committed an act of pure reason and she's never heard of Mr Hawes and Mr Cogan, though the methods of their Royal Humane Society are notorious.[6]

Apply the pipe of a common bellows up one nostril. An assistant will stop the other and the mouth. When the lungs are inflated, a third assistant is to press down on the chest ...

Melville searches around for his bellows. They are not on the hearth. Perhaps his mother has them upstairs? 'No point

---

6 **Royal Humane Society:** *Established in 1774 'for the restoration of human life, when suspended by various kinds of accidental and sudden death, viz. Drowning, strangling, apoplexy, suffocation, and by the noxious vapours of mines, caverns, &c. Intense cold, and the tremendous stroke of lightning.' (Originally, the reward in London was two guineas for attempting a rescue, a further two guineas for successful resuscitation, and a guinea for the pub landlord – a fortune in those days. However, due to the increasing prevalence of scams, rewards were gradually reduced and replaced by medals.)*

in calling for them,' he says. 'The old biddy will have fallen asleep.'

Alternatively, the body may be revived by the kindness of another's breath using a method of mouth-to-mouth inflation ...

Sam stares at the woman's blue lips. He's reluctant to put his mouth there. She may have swallowed a fish or an eel. Suppose the eel jumped out of her mouth and into his? He imagines the muscular slipperiness on his lips, the surprise of it slithering down his throat. Nothing of any great size, just a fingerling, and the muddy aftertaste of it. He wishes they had not caught her. Johnny keeps rubbing, up and down the body, like he's polishing brass.

Fanny the Barometer
Skinner Street, Holborn

The sky above Holborn slides across itself in multiple layers and shades of grey, and grey streaked with purple, and purple streaked with yellow. The clouds piled like dirty blankets trap beneath them the choking piss-stink of the tanneries and the animal stink of the meat market, the human stink of the night soil and the fear stink of the slaughterhouse. And the clouds trap the festering, hopeless stink of the debtors' prisons: Fleet, Newgate, Coldbath, Millbank and Marshalsea. In Holborn, in fact in the whole of London, everyone is sick of clouds.

It is damp but not cold. Dull but not windy. The wind has not blown for days and flags, awnings and washing all hang limp, weathercocks point persistently and stubbornly east. The weather, normally so changeable, has stopped changing.

In the last fifty years or so, the mercury barometer, originally devised by Evangelista Torricelli, has been improved and refined, made simple to interpret by means of a wheel and a pointer, so that even the ladies of the household might now read: STORMY, MUCH RAIN, RAIN, DULL, CHANGE, FAIR, SET FAIR, VERY DRY. By the eighth day of this calm, the pointers seem stuck; everyone wishes for CHANGE, but none is predicted.

At 41 Skinner Street, they used to have a particularly fine example of a weather glass, made by Natalo Aiano, an Italian inventor and skilled glassblower lately of Holborn. It used to hang in the hallway, but it has lately been sold to satisfy a creditor and Mr Godwin pretends that he no longer has any interest in the forecasting of weather. Fanny misses the old instrument, the sheen of its walnut case, the intricacy of its brass work, the craftsmanship of its glass, and she dislikes the void it has left on the wall, but in truth she is herself a barometer. She keenly feels the atmospheric conditions. She feels the cold on her scalp, the damp is an ache in her bones, high pressure makes her anxious, rain overwhelms her with sadness. She stands outside in the street, looks up at the sky, a sky close enough to touch and the colour of a three-day-old bruise, and her grey eyes are brimful of precipitation that holds off – for now.

Density
Skinner Street, Holborn

Troubled by the almost-memory of her mother returning home in damp clothes, Fanny cannot sleep. At least thinking about her mother distracts Fanny from thinking about her sisters, wondering if they are asleep or awake, wondering if they are warm enough, wondering if they ever think of her. In the middle of the sleepless night, she goes quietly down two flights of stairs to Godwin's study, feels along the top of the architrave for his key and unlocks the door. From his bookcase she selects the grief-addled, reckless memoir of her mother, the memoir that caused so much damage to reputations and so much trouble with her Aunts. Fanny reads by candlelight, then she transcribes some passages into her commonplace book. Writing the words somehow makes them more real. Writing comes closer to that feeling of something real, like your fingers closing around something familiar in your pocket. The only sound is the scratch of her pen and the answering scritch-scritch of mice in the wainscoting.

She took a boat and rowed to Putney ...

Unremarkable; Mary Wollstonecraft was, after all, a competent oarswoman.

... it had begun to rain with great violence. The rain suggested to her the idea of walking up and down the bridge, till her clothes were thoroughly drenched and heavy with the wet.

Fanny pauses. Perhaps she has too literal a mind?

... then leapt from the top of the bridge ...

Such drama, a leap like that, how like her. But a mother couldn't be wetter than she would be moments later as the river swallowed her, swelling the wool of her coat, her skirts, her petticoats, filling her boots, unpinning her hair.

... but still seemed to find a difficulty in sinking ...

Ah, dear Mother, Fanny whispers, it's a matter of density. Water cannot be heavier than water. You might have filled your pockets with stones.

After some time she became insensible ...

Not necessarily the same as dead. Perhaps in a faint? Drowning is a slow and painful suffocation — or so it is said.

... having been for a considerable time insensible, she was recovered by the exertions of those by whom she was found.

No, that's not quite right. Fanny scratches out her mistake and inserts a correction.

... exertions of those by whom ~~she~~ <u>the body</u> was found.

Not 'she' but 'the body'. At what point does a person become a body? When does the soul slip out of its mortal pocket?

Then Godwin shamelessly quotes from his late wife's private letters to Gilbert Imlay, where she says, *I was inhumanly brought back to life and misery.* Fanny is gripped by a feeling of something entirely human, nausea perhaps, or panic.

... back to life ...

What if her soul had already slipped away? How might a soul get back into a newly revived body? Fanny shivers and closes the books: the memoir, her own little book – a small thing, not yet one quarter full, bound in dark cloth and fastened with a green ribbon.

... inhumanly brought back to life and misery.

Fanny shivers. These words are indeed her mother's own, written to the feckless cause of her leap. Fanny has read the letters to him, knows these words by heart, carries them around like stones in her pocket.

Bitterly
Skinner Street, Holborn

The house is cold. One frugal fire burns in the parlour, the other grates lie empty. The coal merchant has not delivered; he declares he won't until Godwin settles the account for the last load, and he says that not only hell but also 41 Skinner Street can freeze over before he tips another hundredweight on tick.

London is cold. The year draws to a close and they say that if the temperature continues to fall the Thames will freeze again and there will be a frost fair with skating and puppet shows, cockfighting, gingerbread and hot gin spiced with wormwood. It's something to look forward to, but Fanny doesn't.

If the river does become ice-bound, the eels will sink into the sludge of sour mud on the river's bed, dreaming away their frozen days. Although the eels don't know it, Fanny doesn't know, nobody can know it yet, the river will never completely freeze again and the carnival days of frost fairs are already over.

Fanny has nothing to look forward to. She feels hemmed

in by the house, by its absence of cheer, of funds, of leisure, the continued absence of sisters. When she can escape, she visits her mother's grave – an ugly mausoleum that squats beneath the bare trees amongst the sparse grass, fallen leaves, broken twigs, nut husks. At night she dreams of her sisters, and each morning she wakes to crazy filigree patterns of frost on the inside of the windowpanes, and to a feeling of tapering out, a thinning of her being as if she were evaporating or unravelling. On passing the looking glass in the hallway, she is surprised to see she still has a reflection. Pale, thin, but surprisingly solid.

Fanny feels her aliveness as a restless irritation to be endured, like chilblains. And to be sure, her toes are inflamed and red; they itch with a blazing ferocity.

Part Two: 1815

In which Fanny misses her sisters and the only remedy she finds is in being useful. Mary suffers a tragic loss and becomes increasingly jealous of Claire, and Claire is banished to Lynmouth.

Ah, sister, Desolation is a delicate thing.
(*Prometheus Unbound*, P.B. Shelley)

Sir Bysshe Dies
Nelson Square, Blackfriars
41 Hans Place, Kensington
1 Hans Place, Kensington
Arabella Row, Pimlico

The letter, when it comes, brings news both sad and excellent. At Castle Goring in Sussex there are pennies on old Sir Bysshe's eyes, and at Field Place Shelley's father, the new Sir Timothy, is already closeted with his lawyers discussing probate and unravelling the entails on the estate.[7] In Blackfriars, there is a sense of relief that is naive and premature – it will be more than a twelvemonth before Shelley's current financial predicament eases.

But Shelley is optimistic, so Mary is optimistic. A settlement *will* be reached. They move to better lodgings. Move again. Should have stayed where they were. It will get worse before it will get better. Arguments with the new Sir Timothy over allowances, portions, reversions, mortgages,

---

[7] **Entail:** *A legal restriction placed on property to ensure that it cannot be sold, transferred or bequeathed to anyone outside (the male members of) the family.*

contingencies, taxes and securities dominate their days; the names of lawyers and bankers are always on their lips and in their ears. Meanwhile, creditors circle like buzzards, and some days even those pennies would come in useful.

'How comes it,' asks Claire, as she helps Mary yet again to pack what little they have, plates wrapped in petticoats, journals in pillowslips. 'How comes it,' she asks with her hands on her hips, 'that the heir to a baronetcy and an estate worth more than two hundred thousand pounds still doesn't actually have a pot to piss in?'

January Is the Longest Month

The days of January are short, but the nights begin almost as soon as you sit down to dinner, and candles are priced at two shillings and ten pence the pound. It used to be that after dinner, those long, cosy fireside evenings, Fanny, Mary and Claire would take turns to read aloud, beginning with the Lambs' *Tales from Shakespeare* and progressing to Rousseau, d'Alembert, Paine, and the *Vindications of Rights*. Now Fanny reads alone, reads silently, no one looks up and smiles as she fumbles unfamiliar words.

Janus is the god of transition from one thing to another. From what was once upon a time a family into the cold-shouldered now.

Although her sisters are back, they are not back *home*, and Fanny feels doubly rejected that they should choose to set up house without her. Fanny feels resentment towards Godwin, who will not have them back, and yet she feels closer than ever to him. Better than anyone else, she understands his complicated balancing of opposing tenets, pitting theoretical liberty against real life respectability, though there is always Mrs Godwin to remind him how that translates to food on the table and candles to illuminate your reading.

Meanwhile, January plods on, seemingly for a hundred or more long nights.

Janus is the god of endless corridors.

When they were children, they used to read aloud each evening. It is an excellent habit that Shelley now encourages Mary and Claire to continue. He prescribes texts in Latin and Greek, which they are learning, and the natural sciences, histories and politics, to enlarge and improve their minds. They are to be intellectuals and the almost-equals of men. Mary also rereads her mother's *Letters from Sweden, Norway and Denmark* marvelling at her travelling so far with baby Fanny. Shelley is reading Dunn's *Guide to Modern Finances*. Claire chortles over Henry Mackenzie's *Man of Feeling* and says that the sentimental man in the book – who cries about everything – would do Fanny for a husband.

Janus is the god of war and also of peace because Janus is the god of the beginnings and the endings of conflicts.

But Mary is the equal of Godwin in terms of sheer pig-headed stubbornness. She is adamant that she will not return to Skinner Street. She will forge a new life.

Janus is the god of journeys and of birth.

Before, before everything went wrong, Fanny, Mary and Claire used to read aloud, and the thing with reading aloud is that it saves on candles. Only the one with the book needs good light; everyone else can sit in the fireglow or in the shadows and twiddle their hair.

Janus is the god of doorways. Janus is a two-faced liar.

Being Tickled by Samuel Taylor Coleridge

You remember one evening, after dinner and long past your bedtimes, when you had all three stayed up, listening to the notorious laudanum addict read his Rhyme. You listened to the verses and to the debate that both preceded and followed, until Claire, the youngest, fell asleep with her thumb in her mouth.

'The heart should feed upon reason as a caterpillar feeds on a leaf,' Mr Coleridge said.

Then he made a caterpillar of his index finger and wiggled it along your arm so that you burst out giggling. And Mary cried until he tickled her too.

Gone

You remember being under the table, hidden by the fringed coverlet transforming that corner of the room into any world that you would make it. Mrs Godwin out visiting a friend, and you and your sisters playing house. Mary has borrowed the best cushions and some teacups. You worry you should have stopped her; you must make sure to put them back before they are missed.

'Fanny will be the mother because she's the oldest,' says Mary.

'I'll be the baby,' says Claire. 'You can be the father, Mary.'

Mary never wants to be the father, fathers are boring, She wants to be the baby; she's only a little bit older than Claire and why should Claire get her own way all the time? She says, 'Let's play that there is no father because the father's gone away.'

'Fighting Bony in the war,' says Claire, 'or discovering a continent.'

'Or maybe he just upped and left,' says Mary with a sly glance in your direction.

Mary Wollstonecraft Meets Gilbert Imlay for the First Time
Paris, 1793

'At your service, Ma'am.'

He flips aside his coat-tails and sits in the too-low chair, long shanks commandeering the hearthrug, fingers smoothing the nap of his hat, a look of amusement on his face. Too familiar, almost insolent. And not entirely settled, as if his posture were somehow provisional.

A diplomatic envoy, he says. Hailing from Kentucky, he says. And he stresses the syllables, giving each exactly equal weight: Ken-tuck-kee.

She has heard rumours: some have him down as a boaster, gambler, trickster, speculator, fortune-hunter —

'And I'm a writer, Ma'am. Like yourself.'

— land-grabber, blockade-runner, and philandering interloper.

Like a peddler, he lays out for her the topography of the western territories. His words conjure a utopia of snow-capped mountain ranges with knife-sharp rocks, grizzly bears scooping salmon from cold rivers, white plunging waterfalls, forests like green cathedrals, eagles soaring.

'Pray why, Mr Imlay, have you left the sublime continent?'

He smiles.

The most important life lesson, he thinks, is to know when to quit. Of course, you aim to quit while you're ahead. But sometimes you find yourself behind – enemy lines, the times, closed doors or behind on repayments. . When the situation is *irremediable*, well, it's time to move on. He has, over the years, elevated the timely exit to an art form.

'To travel, Ma'am, to interesting places.'

He keeps his hat in his hands. Britches dusty, a few coins jingling in the pockets, coat well cut, firearm concealed. Finely tooled leather boots. Ostentatious; more pimp than pioneer. But still, charming.

Mary Wollstonecraft is charmed. His tales prompt her to see foreign travel as a new way of thinking, a new-world independence, a revolutionary world view. Despite herself, her ambition, her principles, she imagines devoting her life to this one man.

The Seven-Month Baby
Hans Place, Kensington

The letter says Fanny is needed. The letter galvanises her out of her torpid introspection, dreaming of a father she never really had, a family she no longer has. The letter hauls her from the sludge of her self-pity, jolts her back to life, and she grabs a coat and goes directly.

When she arrives, the curtains are closed; the room has a sour smell. Mary's cheeks burn; her eyes burn – not with a steady flame but with the light of last embers. Fanny hesitates in the doorway. She remembers when Puss had kittens, she saw them slip out, little wet dark parcels in sausage skin, glistening in the candlelight, and Fanny was told she should not touch them for they were not hers. Fanny hovers on the threshold, between then and now.

Next to Mary, on the bed, is the too-early baby wrapped in something. It neither moves nor makes a sound.

'Oh, Mary.'

Mary stares at Fanny with those ember eyes and Fanny feels the pricking of tears.

'It will not feed,' Mary says.

'*It* will not—?'

'Suckle. It will not suckle.'

Fanny goes to the bundle. It is wrapped in a red shawl embroidered with chrysanthemums. The shawl's silken fringe slides across her fingers.

Presently, when Puss was done with her labour, she purred and licked and purred and nuzzled, and the slick parcels became kittens, and she looked as pleased, as pleased as ever a cat might look.

Fanny unfolds the dark red silk, then the soft linen beneath. Mary's baby – red, dark and angry-looking – flinches. Fanny holds her breath, her heart stops, she dies a little at the sight of so pitiful a creature. With its arms and legs exposed, it flexes, reaching out, then relaxes. Fanny looks across at Mary. Mary looks defiantly back, and Fanny wraps it up again.

Puss stretched luxuriantly as the kittens' fur dried and they found their place against her flank.

Fanny instinctively cradles the baby in her arms and eases the crook of her little finger between its lips, and with a surge of joy she feels it turn its head towards her, rooting just a little. 'Try again,' she murmurs to Mary and hands her the parcel. As Mary fumbles with her breast, Fanny moves away to wipe her eyes and draw back the curtains. Below, a door bangs, and she sees Claire and Shelley dance down the steps and out into the street.

They Say Bad News Travels Fast
Holborn to Pimlico

This letter, when it comes, gets misplaced. Mrs Godwin says she has no idea how such a thing might come to pass, and that everybody knows that bad news cannot improve with keeping. Momentarily, Fanny holds the news in the cupped palms of her hands, holds it like it is a bird. Then, before anyone can expressly forbid it, she puts on her coat and hat and is away down Skinner Street and heading south along the riverbank through the intermittent rain, the hem of her skirt darkening as she hastens. She is already five days late.

Now, snowdrops are pushing up through the sleeping soil and the old leaf litter. Fanny hurriedly gathers them: along the side of the road, as she cuts through the churchyards of St John's and St Saviour's, from the garden of an empty house, white, green, fragile, a poor gift. Her gloves are wet through by the time she has amassed a sizeable bunch. Her fingers are numb, wisps of hair plastered to the side of her face. She pushes on through the now steady rain, lengthening her stride to cover the ground between herself and Mary. The baby is already five days cold.

Cuz?
Arabella Row, Pimlico

Mary dreams her baby alive, revived by warmth and by rubbing. The baby breathes, its lips rosebud pink and blistered. Mary sleeps as much as she is able. Sleeps to dream her baby. But increasingly the dream eludes her, and each waking is to a sullen deadness. *They* wake her from her dreaming. Shelley and Claire wake her, bowling in through the front door—

'You did not, you minx, I say, you never did,' brays Shelley.

'I did too. I so did, cuz,' squeals Claire, bursting into the parlour, her bonnet already off, cheeks flushed, ribbons fluttering. 'Oh! Mary, you are up.'

'And sitting in the dark, my love?' says Shelley, moving immediately to the window to draw back the heavy curtains. A moment with his back to her. A moment to make adjustment. Compose himself.

'Cuz', she called him. Not Shelley. Cuz, cousin, kissing cousins.

The light through the window, even filtered through the

grime of the glass, is still too bright. It pierces the gloom of Mary's waking thoughts.

Shelley comes to stand behind her; his cold fingers rub her shoulders, his voice wheedles. 'Could you make us some tea, Mary?' he asks. 'Claire and I, we are that parched, that footsore, we have walked and talked quite the whole day.'

Claire twirls her periwinkle-blue ribbons, looks at Mary from under her lashes.

Stay

Stay (noun 1a): A thing to support and steady something else, e.g., prop, buttress, bracket. A thing that provides support, an object of reliance.

> 'Fanny is a dependable sort,' they say. Godwin depends on you to help with the accounts, with his correspondence, to listen and to agree with him. You take pains to be agreeable. Mrs Godwin leans on you in the managing of the household, the running of the shop, looking after the inventory, dealing with creditors, attending to the more tedious customers, and in a thousand other little tasks. You cannot expect to be carried; you must make yourself useful.

Stay (verb 1a transitive): The act of supporting, sustaining, propping up.

> When Mary and Claire ran away; when Godwin was incapacitated by moral affront and practical helplessness; when Mrs Godwin was at her wits'

end, then they needed you. Then silly sent-away Fanny was recalled to support, sustain and provide spine at Skinner Street.

When Mary and Claire returned to London, but not to Skinner Street, you must not visit. Then you must visit. You must run messages between the two households, You must apologise for Godwin's rudeness, his neediness, his sense of entitlement. You must apologise for Mary's rudeness. For Shelley's fecklessness, his flippancy. You make their excuses, carry more letters, apologise for the letters. When Mary's baby, poor mite, was birthed, you were needed. When the baby died, Mary needed you more. You are kept busy supporting, sustaining and propping up. You are glad, grateful even, to have a purpose.

Fanny the Ambassador
Mr Marshall's house, Somers Town

Claire arrives at the meeting place almost an hour late and wearing an enormous old oilskin coat she says is borrowed from Shelley's friend, Mr Hogg. It has kept her dress reasonably dry, but her shoes and stockings are soaked through, as is her almost-black, waist-length hair, and she wrings that out, looking entirely unrepentant about the puddle she makes on the floor. 'A fine day for drowning a cat, Fanny,' she says with a laugh. 'I'm surprised they let you come out at all.'

Fanny embraces Claire, takes her coat, draws her towards the fire, offers her the best chair. She is anxious to make a success of this meeting, wants to accomplish the thing they have asked her to do. You must be persuasive, they said. You must prise Claire away from the scandal of Mary and her 'situation', they said. Claire is to be offered a fresh start somewhere, so that her reputation may be washed and ironed, so that she, at least, may make something of her life. It is for the best, they said.

Mr Marshall's housekeeper comes in with a tray of tea things, which she sets on a little table before leaving them. They are quite private and on neutral territory, a space of neither Godwin nor Shelley. Just two girls with uncertain futures. They sit close by the fire, Fanny with her hands in her lap, Claire with her feet up on the fender and beginning to steam.

Hesitantly, Fanny begins: 'Claire, it is perhaps … that is, it would be prudent … and maybe …' She takes a breath. 'Maybe you should take care to distance yourself now from Mary and from Shelley, and I have been asked to—'

'I won't go home, I just won't, and that's flat,' Claire says.

'Well, no, not home, not to Skinner Street. Mr Godwin could not have you there. He said—'

'Not have me?' interrupts Claire. 'Not have me home? The old hypocrite!'

'But you see—'

'But absolutely nothing. I declare that Mr Godwin is a shabby sponge who thinks of nothing but his own good standing.'

Fanny is stung. She says stiffly, 'Mr Godwin says, and your mother agrees, they say that this business with Shelley affects all of us, and that people will say—'

'Always such the mouse, Fan. Who cares what people say?'

Fanny feels a cloudburst of refutation condense inside her. How might any person be insensitive to their effect on the world and to the effect of the world on them? How can

Claire throw away her reputation and not care what people say? Fanny cares about what people say about her sisters, what they say about her mother, what they say about Mr Godwin sponging off his friends and his work being worthless. 'I care,' she says quietly.

Claire glares at Fanny; Fanny glares back.

Outside, the rain intensifies, rattling against the windows like handfuls of pea gravel flung in anger, and from somewhere in the darkening sky above comes a great rumble of thunder. Fanny flinches. Claire springs up and stands on the arm of a chair to look out of the clerestory window, hoping to see the fork of light.

'Lord, what a storm. Mary would simply adore this.'

Jealousy
Arabella Row, Pimlico

Remembered from cold Sunday mornings, the numbness of three small behinds on hard benches, the mouthing of commandments, the slap and sting of the calloused hands of the Anglican Sisters of St Paul's: 'Mary Godwin, stop fidgeting and pay attention!'

Mary thought, Mary *had* thought, that jealousy was a fault of God. In Deuteronomy, the jealous God is a consuming fire. In Exodus, 'Jealous' is the name of God, insisting man must have no other.

But now that consuming fire burns her up, and she finds that jealousy is, after all, a fault of woman. She wants to insist that man, that *her* man, must have no other but her.

Jealousy – a pathetic, womanly jealousy – is a low thing. Jealousy is neither capital sin nor cardinal vice. It is not a fierce thing. Not a snorting Minotaur pounding through the labyrinth. Not a wronged creature driven by rage, racing across Arctic wastes. Jealousy is a mean and dirty reptile of a thing that slinks on its belly.

And she doubts herself, doubts her feelings, doubts the evidence of her eyes and ears. Suspicion eats away. How to banish such suspicions? How not to feel displaced? Shelley stays up talking with Claire, Shelley is out with Claire, Shelley and Claire, Claire & Shelley, until Mary cannot bear to write her sister's name in her journal and resorts to *Shelley and 'his little friend'*. When at last she explains to him how wretched this jealousy of her own sister makes her feel, how she longs for *absentia Clariae*, Shelley tells her this: spend more time with Hogg, write to Hogg, sleep with Hogg.

And she will not. Although she has written.

The Great Chain of Being, As Explicated by Mr Samuel Taylor Coleridge
Skinner Street, Holborn

In all natural things there is an order, from this to that, from before to after, life to afterlife. Everything has its time and its place. A Great Chain of Being. The notorious old laudanum addict had explained it to Fanny (and to Mary too, but she hadn't been paying attention, and to Claire, who had fallen asleep with her thumb in her mouth).

All things in nature have an order, from the least to the greatest. At the bottom are the leastest things, like pebbles and rocks, and it seems incredible to Fanny that a mountain of solid rock – specifically granite – solid granite, an unimaginable vastness of it, like the mountain behind Aunt Lydia's house at Pentredevy in Wales, should be a lesser thing than say, a bird. And that salt, a useful preservative, is less than an ant, which is nothing but a pest.

It's all a matter of animation, Coleridge said. Rocks and minerals, being inanimate, belong lower down, then comes vegetable matter, all the plants and trees of the world and its oceans ranked according to complexity, that is to say, importance. Is that to say, value? Where oak trumps moss and strawberries trump plankton. Then, above all the trees and vegetables, comes the lowest of the animate matter, the animalcules, amoebae, lice, mites, spiders, then little fish, big fish, hedgehogs, cats, and on through all the sentient beings of the animal kingdom, arranged according to their complexity, importance, value. Horses, Fanny thinks, must be near the top.

Then comes man, which is to say, woman, so firstly, Adam's rib,[8] and all her daughters, and above them Adam and all the sons of Adam. It had been thought that kings with their divine right were placed directly above man, but times were changing and Mr Coleridge said a king was not so elevated these days and that it was widely acknowledged – in this more enlightened era – that in fact poets come next. So next, the poets, a superior class of man with particular refined powers of imagination. A human pyramid of poets each endeavouring to hold and support those that stand on their shoulders, and *their* shoulders, and on *their* shoulders, and Virgil teetering on the apex with Dante and Milton bellyaching just below.

What comes above the poets? Fanny might well wonder, having seen a poet or two but never the next or yet more lofty and sublime strata. Those realms are occupied by

---

*8 **Adam's Rib:** Eve, or more broadly, woman. In the Bible (Genesis 2:21) God created first Adam, then from Adam's rib he made Eve, a companion to be always at Adam's side.*

angels. There are cherubim and seraphim, guardian angels with special duties, then angels proper, then archangels. The nearer the top, the fewer there are. Named archangels are rare and Coleridge could think of only three: Gabriel, Michael and Raphael. Fanny imagines them flying above the poets on cheap tinsel wings.

Then God.

Modernisation
Snow Hill, Holborn

But put God aside for a minute. There is change afoot. A paradigm shift in mankind's understanding of the world. Out with the sad trash as the old ways are left behind. Out with the theories of humours, of choler, bile, spleen, out with bismuth and mercury. In with the newly discovered modern elements, hydrogen and magnesium. Out with phlogiston, in with oxygen. Life is no longer a matter of alchemy but of chemistry, and they say that soon we will have the cure for death — just as soon as they discover the cause of life.

All along Snow Hill, handbills have been posted for a lecture on electricity to be held in Covent Garden. Fanny stops to read and wonders if she might go. She knows she won't. Alone, at night, and squander a shilling on a magic lantern show? But still. She wonders about the spark.

She wonders about a lot of things these days. As she goes about her errands, keeping busy, being useful, she wonders. About God. Shelley says there is no God. But he could be wrong. It turns out that he is wrong about a great many things. He strings words together elegantly enough, but their meanings do not hold, or at least not in the real world. He stands on one leg, like a stork or a heron, and Fanny believes he is possibly the stupidest of all the clever men she has ever met.

So Fanny wonders about God. About souls. About the spark. About her mother. She wonders how come the river didn't kill her mother but a baby did. About how come Mary's baby just stopped living. Alive one minute and dead the next. But there is little time for unravelling these thoughts; she must hurry home with iron gall ink for Godwin and the *London Gazette* for Mrs Godwin, who will admonish her for dawdling. She quickens her pace.

Learning How to Make Wise Choices Only Helps When You Have a Choice

You remember when Mary was five, Claire four and you were eight, a lady came to visit and brought a basket of peaches grown in her hothouse. You were allowed to take one each. Ah, the feel of the furred skin, the curve, the scent. Mary said hers was sour. She snatched yours and bit into it. Juice dribbled down her chin; she grinned. You said, oh, that's not fair, you chose first, you had your pick.

Mr Godwin said nothing until the lady had gone, then he was vexed with Mary, though he loved her best, and would naturally have preferred her to have the sweetest fruit.

You remember how Mary took her scolding about choices and consequences, pale, without a word, then when no one was looking, she smacked you in the mouth.

Bruised lips lisp.

Mary laughed.

Now Mary is seventeen and gone; you are twenty-one and still at home. Nobody brings gifts of peaches. Ladies with hothouses don't visit Skinner Street these days. The

Godwins cannot afford to buy peaches. These are consequences of choices made. The Godwins cannot afford to keep you for ever. That is also a consequence.

Has Fanny a choice? There are few options for unmarried women of respectable if rather bookish upbringing but small means. The professions are not yet open to them. They have not the skills to be hatters, the temperament for the stage, the brawn of a washerwoman, the desperation of the streetwalker. If such women must earn their keep, and so often they must, they might become a paid companion, perhaps to a disagreeable old lady whose friends and relations claim to be too busy to attend to her. They might become a governess, a difficult position, at ease in neither the parlour nor the kitchen. They might teach in a dame school, teach dates and spellings to other people's children. The choices are limited. And limiting. One whiff of impropriety and doors close.

Speak when you are spoken to.

A companion or governess must be of good character and unmarried, unlikely to marry, perhaps unmarriageable, probably unlovable. A spinster, spinner, spider.

Cold mouth aches.

Plain Cake
London, various parts

Aunt Eliza and Aunt Everina are in London on one of their occasional visits. The cautious and respectable elderly Aunts will navigate the unfamiliar streets attending to business affairs and making some small but necessary purchases. Fanny will accompany them. 'This is your best option,' Mrs Godwin said at breakfast. 'Be sure to make a good impression.' Even though she does her utmost to be of service, Fanny can't expect to stay at Skinner Street for ever. She must soon make her own way in the world, and she might perhaps go to Dublin to teach in the Aunts' school. Fanny knows well enough what is expected of her, and besides, they are her mother's sisters; she wills herself to love them.

All day, Fanny waits on the Aunts' pleasure. She attends, makes herself useful, carefully conserves her opinions. Her blotting paper ears absorb the sharpness of Everina, the woolliness of Eliza. And where the streets are narrow, they walk in file.

They visit the dingy offices of a Mr Sturridge, where Aunt Everina deals briskly with matters pertaining to their inherited interests in some properties on Primrose Street: repairs and renewals, rent reviews. The revenue, though meagre, is an essential supplement to their school income. They move on. Fanny, who is herself a burden, a parcel, carries all the smaller parcels. Six pairs of thick worsted stockings, two bottles of Godfrey's Cordial, twelve yards of grosgrain binding, a copy of Harrington's Almanac. Aunt Eliza dithers over the purchase of some gull-grey gloves that cannot be got in Dublin. 'Not for love nor money,' she says.

When the Aunts' errands are all run and Aunt Eliza declares herself quite puffed out, they stop to take tea. There is cake: seed cake, nothing fancy. Fanny feels the caraway seeds in her mouth, wonders if she has them in her teeth. Aunt Eliza certainly does. Eliza smiles, pats Fanny's arm and asks, 'Have you heard from your sisters at all, Fanny dear?' Fanny has, but knows a lie will serve best here, so she says no, and Aunt Everina says, 'Well, it's a great pity *they* were not plainer in looks – a deal of trouble might have been spared.' Then in the silence that follows that remark, Everina says, 'I don't know why people speak so highly of London – it is disappointingly shabby,' and Eliza helps herself to another slice.

The Nature of Life, and What Happened to the Newt
Putney Bridge

They are out together, Fanny, Mary, Claire. Walking to the Botanical Gardens, where the new hothouses are open to the public. This is the first time in a long time that they have walked together arm in arm. At first their strides are mismatched, their steps contrapuntal. They begin to speak all at once, then not at all. Mary squeezes Fanny's arm. Claire makes a little skip-step.

'*Lavender's blue, dilly dilly*,' she sings, and they giggle, and they are all again sisters, of a sisterhood that might transcend the obstacles of men.

'Is it true,' asks Mary, 'that you will have to go for a schoolmistress, Fanny?'

'It is not yet decided. I must wait to hear from our aunts in Dublin. But please don't let's talk of that, not on such a day as this.'

'I'm sure you will make an excellent schoolteacher,' says Claire. 'You know almost everything.'

'What do you know of Mr Abernethy?' asks Mary. 'Shelley has lately had his nose buried in his book.' The book contains transcripts of Mr Abernethy's *Physiological Lectures* given to the Royal College of Surgeons. Mary will read them next.

'The physician who makes claim to understand the nature of life? I've heard Mr Coleridge mention him,' says Fanny.

'I've heard that Mr Abernethy is exceedingly rude to his patients,' said Claire.

'Hmm,' says Mary. 'I have not yet read Mr Abernethy's theories of the vital spark, but Shelley is certainly a devotee of his biscuits.'

'His *revolting* biscuits,' says Claire.

They laugh, and from the corner of her eye Fanny notices how Mary puts her hand protectively around the slight convexity of her belly where perhaps another baby already grows in the space so recently vacated.

'And then there is Mr Abernethy's erstwhile protégé,' says Fanny.

'Ah, yes, a new voice. I believe Mr Lawrence is something of a scandal,' says Mary.

Claire is inclined to admire scandalous behaviour if only because she too is deemed scandalous. Look! She is not wearing any stays. Her dress catches in the breeze, pressing the muslin against her flat belly. Fanny has no problem with the unorthodoxy of Mr Lawrence's ideas but wishes Claire would button up her coat. Passers-by look askance at the three young women, arm in arm, striding out, debating matters of life and death, matters obviously better left to men. Claire smirks at their glances.

Mr Lawrence, a materialist, has caused umbrage amongst the old vitalists with his lectures, also delivered to the Royal College of Surgeons. Abernethy had declared matter inherently inert, incapable of organisation. Lawrence now says the opposite. Life, he says, is not predicated on the addition of some random spark from some immaterial dimension of say, angels.

'Well, anyway, it is true what he says about newts,' says Fanny. 'Growing a new tail if by mishap they lose their old one.' And privately she wonders, can humans grow a new soul if they lose their old one, perhaps in a drowning accident?

'Do you remember the newt we kept for a pet?' asks Mary.

'Oh Lord. Yes!' says Claire.

'Poor newt,' says Fanny, and they fall silent as they remember how the newt somehow found its way into the boiling copper and got washed with the bed sheets, and all the trouble that caused.

'Do you think newts have a soul?' asks scandalous Claire, and Fanny and Mary stop and stare at her.

River
Thames Embankment

Fanny takes her leave of her sisters, squeezes Mary's hand, and in the squeeze she conveys her message: look after yourself, look after the new seed that grows in you, the thing you have not yet told anyone about, try to eat properly, never mind Shelley's faddy vegetable diets, he is an idiot. Eat meat, drink milk, rest, don't worry, send for me whenever I can be useful.

She strikes for home along the river bank, watching the barges labouring upstream on the incoming tide. Bricks, cement, coal, horse fodder. Some barges, Fanny notes, are manned by women. She watches the bargees in their black skirts, she watches them steer, haul on ropes, hoist red-ochre sails, call out in a language or dialect foreign to her ear. Brawny, broad-leather-belted, sleeves rolled up. A hard life? she wonders.

She thinks of her mother rowing a small boat to Putney Bridge, there to commit an act of pure reason. Fanny doesn't for one hypothetical instant imagine her mother to have been wrong at that precise and long-past moment. Only later, in an as yet unimagined future, could it turn out to have been wrong. Wrong because without her mother's continued existence there could be no Mary, and a world without Mary is unthinkable. But Fanny does not blame her mother. When neither reason nor feeling can be counted on, how can a woman anticipate the twists and turns of life? Such twists surely mean that any choice is suspect, could turn out to be wrong; every act, every word is potentially a misstep.

Fanny looks away from the busy commerce of the river, away from its mudbanks, flotsam, hufflers and wherrymen.[9] She looks away from the river as if she might, thereby, look away from the thought - the thought that has begun to bother her so much – as if the thought is located there, in the water, brackish, tidal. A thought that has begun fermenting. Not in her head, nor between the mudbanks, but here, in the pit of her gut.

She looks to the buildings, shades her eyes with her hand, scanning the skyline. So many tall buildings as the city expands, and she tries not to think about the river, like a vein, where the outgoing tide will take away the rubbish, the night soil, horse dung, ash, bones, rags. Everything the city has no use for.

---

*9 **Huffler:** Casual labourer who hangs about at river bridges to assist with taking down sails and masts. **Wherryman:** person who operates a commercial inland craft transporting goods or passengers.*

The Letter That Comes
Skinner Street, Holborn

The letter that comes, comes when Fanny is out. It lies in wait for her, its fastidious script sloping by a consistent number of degrees, patiently biding its time.

The letter from Aunt Everina and Aunt Eliza, now back in Dublin, belatedly wishes Fanny many happy returns for her birthday. It complains about the properties in Primrose Street, complains about the weather, complains about rheumatism (Everina), a quinsy (Eliza), and the shingles, and lumbago. It complains about the late payments from their pupils, the difficulty of making ends meet. It hints darkly about the ongoing cost of damage to reputation, damage done by girls who do not know their place, girls who do not stay put. It complains about the poor taste and careless excesses of a number of their Dublin acquaintances. It does not send for Fanny. Indeed, the letter suggests no plans for her future.

When Does the Soul Leave the Body?

Slighted yet slightly relieved, Fanny tries to keep busy and to be of use. She applies a paste of vinegar and soda ash to the candlesticks, then buffs it off with a rag. The thought that has begun to bother her lands like a fly, buzzes about, then lands again. Of course, her father *had* just upped and left, causing her poor rejected mother to throw herself in the river. But the thought is this. If her mother *was* drowned, and brought back to life, what then happened to her soul? Had it not yet left her? Or did it just slip back in? Like a hand into a pocket. Is that the way it works?

The brass begins to gleam.

Absentia Clariæ
Lynmouth, Devon

As Wellington and Bonaparte prepare to settle long-running differences, there is, at last, a point of agreement between the Godwin and the Shelley households. Mrs Godwin is still trying to persuade Claire that she should be distanced from the scandal of Mary and Shelley. Mary too, wants Claire gone. It is all she wants, she says, and so Claire is sent away – to Lynmouth, where Shelley once sailed his paper boats.

The landlady of the boarding house is a rotund woman with a smile like a snare. She feels the stuff of Claire's sleeve to gauge its worth and disguises the gesture as affection. 'I'm sure you will be comfortable here, my little bud. We shall get along together very nicely,' she says.

Claire feigns exhaustion, wills herself pale, and asks to be shown straight to her room. She is not sure she wants to get along.

'Ah, 'tis a long journey, my little bud, most wearisome, I'm sure.' The woman pats Claire again, and Claire thinks that if she continues to treat her like a lapdog, she shall bark and bite.

From the gabled window of her room, Claire can see the harbour and most of the town. There's really not much to see. A few streets of jumbly little cottages either side of the river, many in a state of disrepair – piglets run squealing in and out over the threshold of one – and the river tumbles into the harbour and snakes through the mud, where the tide is out and a few shabby fishing boats lie on their sides, making perches for gulls.

Claire unpacks her books and paper, and seated at a little secretaire in the corner, she writes at once to Fanny to tell her she has arrived safely, and to tell her how quaint and fascinating the place is, how enviable her independence, her freedom. Poor Fanny, still at home, minding the shop and running up and down the staircases, at the beck-and-call of Mrs Godwin. She boasts to Fanny of how splendid are the opportunities here, to walk and read, entirely at her leisure, how *completely* splendid. As her pen scratches across the paper, Claire becomes aware of a silent dampness settling on her. A loneliness she has never felt before.

What Animates the Living?
Skinner Street, Holborn

What separates man from the lesser animals? What separates man from oysters, from the eels in the river, Claire's newt, the mice in the wainscoting or Mrs Godwin's idle cats? Fanny watches the cats sunning themselves, watches the light make a sundial of their dusty flanks as they flaunt themselves in the shop window and forty-wink away their days.

What animates the living? Erasmus Darwin supposes a living principle — a spirit that stimulates the body. Although he can neither see nor explain it, he can witness it at work in the circulation of the blood, the inhalation of air, the refluxes of the digestive system, reflexes of the nervous system. The fact that he can't explain it is no bar to its existence. It is *a provisionally inexplicable explicative device*, like Mr Newton's gravity.

Fanny has stayed up half the night reading a book by Mr Hume, a thinker rather than a scientist, who thinks of a secret power. When there are no customers in the shop, which is most of the day, Fanny reads Dr Stephenson's explanation that what differentiates the quick from the dead is Heat.

Obviously not just the sun's heat Fanny reasons, for a stone can be warmed but has no life. Is the special heat caused by friction? some of the vitalists ask. No, says Stephenson, 'Heat' is produced by a fermentation-like process, and the smallest residue of it can restart the heart and thus restore life to the apparently dead.

A man whose name Fanny cannot remember has declared it to be gas.

Upstairs above the shop there is an argument in progress, one of the habitual arguments about time, or noise, or money. Fanny blocks her ears; she dreads catching a mention of her name. She makes herself as quiet as she can be, small as she can be, as translucent as she can be. In spite of herself she smooths one of the cats.

The cats have no place here, they are not supposed to be in the bookshop, certainly not in the shop window. Now the tortoiseshell one rouses, stands and stretches, then proceeds to cough. Long furred and undergroomed, it suffers hairballs, and the convulsions of its body remind Fanny of the long-ago unfortunate Puss, of her madness, of her abrupt end.

A man called Cullen declares that life lingers after the heart ceases to beat. There is, he says, a condition of the nerves, an irritability, that might remain a while, and if provoked, can trigger the heart to beat again. Poor Puss, drowned in a sack in the river, her fur sodden, her irritability completely soothed.

Fanny is thankful that with the improvement in the weather, her chilblains have cleared up.

A man called Galvani has been giving public demonstrations where he makes dead things move. Dead frogs dance. He says it is electricity. Fanny would like to go to one of these demonstrations, would like to see for herself the spark. But a frog dancing is a very different thing to a person. Then her train of thought is broken by the cat. The cat – not troubling itself with uncovering the secret of life – at last retches up its hairy slime, then settles back down to wipe its whiskers with the back of its paws.

Pantisocracy
Lynmouth, Devon

Pantisocracy is an inkhorn word for a pipe dream of equality made up by men. Men who already have almost everything. Shelley explained it as a new and better way of living, governed by parity and egalitarianism, but still it's just a word made up by poets and dreamers.

Claire wanders along the empty shoreline. She wanders most days at low tide, there is so little else to do.

There was some talk, back then, when the word was new minted, about the perfectibility of man – of mankind, you understand, not the perfection of actual men. No, not that. They talked of rational benevolence, of share and share alike. For the women who were to be shared out amongst them like so many slices of cake, things were obviously less than perfect.

She stoops now and then to pick up a pebble or a shell.

Shelley seems to know all about them, those old Pantisocracy poets, the ones who married the sisters. He would sit up at night with his friends, sometimes with Peacock, sometimes with Hogg, jawing by the fire about how it would have been such a fine thing if only those old codgers had had more gumption, had seen it through and gone to the Americas, made a new and better society.

'Claire, bring us another bottle.'

'Claire, is there any cheese?'

Some nights, in the glow of the firelight, Claire would sit with them, perched on Peacock's knee, or perhaps on the floor by the hearth with her head in Shelley's lap and his fingers in her hair. And Hogg with that big broad head of his nodding, but inside it he'd probably be dreaming of Mary, who was already gone to bed.

The sand peters out and the shoreline becomes rocky and slippery with kelp and sea lettuce.

Those nights by the fire, talking and talking of the old poets, of Coleridge, Southey, Lovell, their names an incantation: Coleridge, Southey, Lovell. But Shelley, Peacock and Hogg, they never said the sisters' names. They didn't know the sisters' names, no more than they would know the names of dogs or slices of cake. Edith, Sara, Mary, Martha.

She turns and walks back the way she came.

Shelley's first wife, Harriet, has a sister called Eliza, who used to live with them. Back then, Shelley and Hogg were already talking of such a Pantisocratic utopia, of sharing in that way. Shelley would have willingly shared Harriet with Hogg, but Harriet was most unwilling; she had threatened to cut off Hogg's baubles if he laid a finger. But anyway, two sisters: Harriet and Eliza.

At Skinner Street, when they first met him, Shelley was

flirtatious. Three sisters! Such sisters! he would say. Fanny, Mary, Claire. One would never have been enough.

As she rejoins the pathway that leads back to the harbour and the hateful boarding house, Claire flings her pebbles and shells towards the water.

And then, all living on top of one another in various lodgings, and those nights sitting by the fire; Shelley and Peacock and Hogg. Shelley loves Hogg and would give him his last sixpence. He encourages Mary to be kind to him. Mary tries; she found some comfort in Hogg's attentiveness after the poor seven-month thing died, but in truth she loves only Shelley, and now she has what she wants, she has him all to herself.

How could we all have been so stupid?

Underdone
Skinner Street and Bishopsgate

The year rolls on and the streets begin to fill with soldiers returning from the war, bedraggled, somehow incomplete, without work and dependent on charity. The Godwins have a new cook, a pinch-faced woman missing a finger on her right hand; she does not take well to Mrs Godwin's style of instruction and will not last long. She will leave at Michaelmas with a silver carving fork (in lieu of wages) concealed in the sleeve of her coat, but for now she comes in four days a week. Towards the end of the new cook's second and penultimate week the Godwins have a guest to dine with them, no one important, which is a blessing as the beef is underdone and Godwin sends it back to the kitchen only half-eaten.

In the morning, Fanny wraps the remains of the rib joint in a clean muslin cloth and leaves the house with it concealed beneath her coat. She is aware that her position within the household, as the daughter of neither Godwin nor Mrs Godwin is precarious, is increasingly precarious.

She is expected to be frugal, grateful and of service and this makes her appropriation of the meat – though not as bad as stealing the silver – a dubious action. But necessary.

The person Fanny loves most is in need, and Fanny knows the meat will help. She is away early, before anyone else is about, and with her rare booty scurries through the streets. Shelley, who has been up half the night reading Rousseau, sleeps late.

'Mary, you are not eating enough, you need something to feed your blood.'

And it is true. Living on nothing but vegetables and biscuits, Mary is pale and thin, her hair is dull, her skin sallow, she is anaemic, a ghost, a pregnant ghost. Shyly, Fanny unwraps her gift and watches with satisfaction as Mary's eyes widen.

'Oh, Fanny,' Mary says. She takes the contraband and without delay or ceremony begins to bite and gnaw and chew. Her teeth rip the flesh, the juices trickle down her chin, she licks her lips, and there is something monstrous about her eating. But as she savours the feast, her eyes feather shut. Like the Magdalene, thinks Fanny, and blushes from the pleasure of watching her sister eat. Mary chews steadily, and when she has finished she wipes her mouth on the muslin, wraps up the picked-clean bone and hands it back to Fanny. 'So good,' she whispers.

George Blood
Kennington, London

Fanny has always known she was named after her mother's great friend, Fanny Blood, now long since dead, and really, childbirth kills more women than war kills men. Fanny Blood's brother George writes to say he will be in London and wishes to call at Skinner Street. George is a remarkably stupid man and Godwin spares him little time.

Deputised to be hospitable, Fanny warms to the old buffoon who speaks so highly of her mother, who he calls 'a superior being' when he and Fanny walk to the grave at Pancras. He declares himself keen to make the acquaintance of the daughters of the marvellous Mary Wollstonecraft and seems not at all put out that he must make do with just the one.

He relates many little memories of the old days when Mary Wollstonecraft and Fanny Blood were as close as sisters, of their great love for one another. 'Your mother was a tremendous teacher, explaining really difficult things, you know?' he says.

'What things?'

'Mathematics, politics, women, all the important things in life.'

George's encomium chisels away at Fanny's cloud, and the following day they walk to Kennington, where a travelling fair has set up in a field. 'It looks rowdy,' she says.

George takes her arm, and they plunge into the melee. Fanny wishes she'd said something else, annoyed that George Blood might misthink her timid. She is not afraid of the street entertainers, nor the noisy throng, the beggars and bawds, pickpockets, cutpurses, garlick-eaters, flashers and fops. London is her home.

They watch a Mr Punch puppet show, a brass band and two salamanders eating fire. George eats a hot potato. When he has wiped his mouth and declared himself reinvigorated, they wander on through the crowds and find themselves at the tent of a chiromancer.

'Oh deary,' says George, 'I'm too old to have enough future left to be worth sixpence – but you must have yours told.' He pays, and to oblige him, though she believes it to be nonsense, she enters the tent, where a Turk in flowing saffron robes and a blackened face seats her at a card table, takes her slightly clammy hand in his leathery one and traces the creases of her palm. He tells her that she will have a long life and at least six children but must take care of her liver lest it plague her. Fanny draws back her hand and wishes she might wash it. She is not sure she wants children of her own. She stands unsteadily, smooths her skirt and dips out through the flap of his tent, back to George Blood, who is

117

idly wondering what his life would be like if he had been less timid, if he had told Fanny's mother how he felt about her.

A Lecture on Electricity, the Gasses and the Phantasmagoria
Fyne Court, Quantock Hills

Between the trees at Fyne Court, Mr Andrew Crosse has strung yards and yards of copper wire. He is a fanatical-poetical man, interested in the properties of statical electricity and atmospherical electricity; they say he has the power to summon thunder and lightning from the sky. Squirrels, caring nothing for all of that, make unauthorised use of the tree-to-tree trapeze wires. Now, nuts are ripening, leaves falling, the architectural structure of the trees becomes increasingly visible, and the weather is changing, yielding valuable data. Crosse walks the length and breadth of his estate, examining his wires, checking on the levels in his fifty jars of as yet unpatented acid solution, checking on the twenty-inch brass cylinder that he turns over and over with a handle. He scribbles in his notebook: *A mackerel sky, dampish, some drifting mist. [41¾]. Negative, decreasing, 3 minutes. Positive. Mushrooms. Edible?*

Locally, they say he is a wizard. Locally, they say he beats his wife, which is why she has a face that would curdle milk. Locally, they say he can cure rheumatism, and the old and the cranky from miles around apply to Fyne Court to take the electric cure and they swear it works. And his reputation is spreading. Already, he has collaborated with Mr Singer on his book, *Elements of Electricity and Electro-Chemistry*. Already, he is known to be a capital fellow and a genial host; his acquaintances include Michael Faraday, Humphry Davy and Robert Southey. Already, he is admired for his experimental works in the new branches of the natural sciences, but much less so for his doggerel poetry.

Not yet, but in the near future, before this year is out, Andrew Crosse will deliver a lecture at Garnerin's London lecture rooms on the subject of harnessing electricity from thunderclouds. Mary Godwin will be in the audience paying rapt attention, and she will wonder what use might be made of this power. Years later, Andrew Crosse will meet Byron's (as yet unborn) daughter, Ada Lovelace; she will visit him at Fyne Court, she will have an affair with his son John, and John will introduce Ada to betting on the horses. Andrew Crosse will go on to experiment with crystallisation and make some remarkable observations. He will become discredited due to a claim he never actually made, a claim to have created, *ex nihilo*, minuscule electrical animals – and that is blasphemous; only the Almighty creates life, and man should not meddle. In the end though, these animalcules turn out to be cheese mites accidentally contaminating his experiment. But none of that has happened yet. For now, the quick go about their business, dead things stay dead, and the squirrels scamper along his high wires.

Inky Fingers

Letters fly like paper birds with requests, behests, sketches, recipes for cough cures, apologies, rebukes, arms'-length best wishes – as if wishes were horses and beggars might ride. Please remit at your earliest convenience. My dearest, sincerely yours. Letters with advice, reproach, news, no news, promises made and kept or not kept, perhaps never explicitly made in the first place. Letters are written, copied, posted, anxiously awaited, delivered, opened, read, replied to. Letters are kept, burnt, shared, hoarded, noted in journals, hidden in drawers. Some letters are lost in the post.

Godwin writes to Shelley. Shelley writes to Claire. Claire writes to Fanny. Fanny writes to Mary. Mary writes to Shelley. Shelley writes to Godwin. Fanny writes back. Shelley writes to Mary. Mary writes to Fanny. Fanny writes to Claire. And Claire writes to Byron.

Part Three: 1816

Sick of playing second fiddle, Claire sets her sights on a poet of her own: Lord Byron, the most talented and disreputable of poets.

'You know that odd-headed girl? I never loved her nor pretended to love her – but a man is a man – and if a girl of eighteen comes prancing to you at all hours of the night – there is but one way'.
(Byron, letter to his half-sister Augusta)

The repercussions affect everyone.

Old Year/New Year
Skinner Street and Bishopsgate

On the last night of the old year, it is traditional to repay debts and sweep the ashes from the fireplace. Fanny does what she can. As darkness falls, the city streets become noisy with revellers. A cacophony of ancient customs and the last hoorah of Christmas. There are Wrenboys, the Kentish Hooden Horses, the Broad Bull's Head, the Mari Llwyd, the mollies and mummers, all abroad, some bent on mischief. Others follow the northern custom of first-footing with parcels of coal and bread, a twist of salt, and in return perhaps a penny, perhaps a drink. Some are already in their cups. The apprentices have work in the morning and will have thick heads.

Over in Bishopsgate, Mary and Shelley have guests. Hogg and Peacock are there, Claire too – an *entente cordial* between her and Mary, for the festive season at least. Shelley has been attentive of late, and Mary feels more secure, though as she lumbers about she envies Claire's waistline. Claire is glad of the company, glad to be back with Mary and Shelley, but growing tired of a tedious conversation about Polyphemus; she sits alone playing patience.

In Skinner Street, there is a good fire; Godwin and Mrs Godwin doze in its glow. Fanny feels restless and wishes she could run headlong through the streets with a horse's head. At five to midnight, she wraps her shawl around her shoulders and steps outside. The sky is clear, a perfect firmament, she thinks, and as she waits for the bells to ring in the new year she wishes for her sisters and wonders, might Mary's new baby be born this night? But Mary's baby is high and snug; he will not come yet.

Fanny gazes up at the constellations, looking for Orion, knowing that the star on the left of his belt is her star. Mary's is the middle one and Claire's is on the right. She remembers Godwin saying the names of the stars, and that the name of Mary's star means pearls and hers means a girdle, and she puts her hands to her waist and feels beneath her dress the stiffness of her mother's stays.

Then the bells of every tower and every steeple begin to peal their complex carillons, their Plain Bob Doubles and Reverse Canterburies, the sounds cascading over and over, and as the peals at last begin to ebb, all the clocks of the city start to strike and chime the hour, revellers let fly their squibs, and the ships on the river blow their horns, and the new year begins.

Fresh Meat
Skinner Street, Holborn

First, the butcher sends his boy. The boy scratches his ears, a nervous tic, and he presents the overdue bill.

'Goodness me, the price of pork!' says Fanny. 'I'm sure Mr Godwin will settle up at the end of the month.' And she keeps her foot against the door. He's only a boy after all.

On Tuesday, the boy is back. 'The thing is,' he says, scratching furiously, 'my master says it be long past the end of the month and your Master Godwin mun pay his bill today.'

'Mr Godwin is out,' says Fanny. 'Call again tomorrow when you bring the chickens.' And she closes the door in his face.

On Wednesday, the boy brings spatchcock chickens and a revised inventory of the amount owing.

Thursday's mutton arrives with a message that there is to be no more credit.

Friday, Mrs Godwin comes over all Catholic and wants fish. Fanny takes up her basket and goes to the market on Snow Hill.

Then, on Saturday morning, the butcher himself comes. He is a large man with a bristling moustache like a worn scrubbing brush and remarkably pink hands. Fanny does not like the look of him and tries to keep her foot against the door, but he barges past her, demanding to see Mr Godwin. 'If this debt is not discharged today, your fine Mr Godwin will end up in the sponging house,' he says.[10]

Fanny leaves the butcher standing in the rear hallway. He loiters respectfully with his hat in those large pink hands. For all his bluster, he's only a tradesman after all.

She hides around the corner; she hates having to deal with Godwin's creditors, hates the duplicity and the prevarication, but it is the way of her world. She counts in her head until five minutes have passed, then returns and delivers the lie: Mr Godwin is not at home. The butcher's eyes graze over her as if he imagines nuzzling his moustache along her collarbone. He mistakes her for the maid – she is in her apron, she has been keeping busy, making herself useful. 'Shin beef,' he says.

'I beg your pardon?'

---

10 Sponging house: A house to which debtors are taken to await committal to prison, where, according to Dr Johnson, the bailiffs 'sponge upon them or riot at their cost'.

'I've some lovely shin beef, could bring it round tomorrow, it's my day off. Or chitterlings?'

'Yes, the beef. But be sure to add it to the account,' she says and herds him out of the door.

Godwin peers over the upstairs banisters. 'Good girl, Fanny,' he says.

If a Woman Wrote a Letter ...
Arabella Row, Pimlico

If a woman who was rejected by those who should love her, and forced to live alone in London, in seedy lodgings, dependent on handouts, with little to do but walk through the streets and the parks and dawdle in churches and galleries and any free attractions to stave off boredom, and think about the circumstances in which she was not allowed home to her mother, and had been sent away from the impossible *ménage* of her sainted sister and her skylark poet, might such a woman realise that she should, under no circumstances at all, have settled for second best, or for second place, or for second anything? Might she not become restless?

If such a woman, a restless woman who feels that certain privileges and agency are practically a birthright and certainly no less than her due, were to decide that what she wants is not a half-share of a spindle-shanked skylark poet, what she actually wants is a poet of her own – and it is only reasonable for her to want such a thing – might she not set her cap at a more famous poet, a wealthier poet, a titled poet, a poet famed for his glowering dark looks and wild spirit, so that she might imagine saying to her stepsister, 'Well, Mary, my dear, who is envious now?'

So, if a woman, a restless woman, convinced that her rights and agency *as a woman* were entirely vindicated, wanted a poet (the famous, wealthy, titled, glowering poet) of her very own, how might such a thing be managed? If she had no one to introduce her, nothing to recommend her but her alluring looks, her creamy skin and her own dark curls, and also a figure that draws admiring glances, and if she had nothing to lose, quite literally nothing, and if she was resolute, and also a little reckless (with the hammering heart that such an endeavour might occasion), might she not decide to take matters into her own hands? If she furnished herself with paper and ink, if she penned him a letter, what might be the worst that could happen?

In *Loco Parentis*

Before your sisters, when you were Fannikins, and it so happened that your mother was having her portrait painted – it hangs now over the mantelpiece in the study and Mr Godwin is excessively proud of it, but of course his second wife mutters that Mr Opie has caught your mother's lazy eye exactly, and, of course, it is entirely excusable that a second wife might fixate on such a detail, for how else should she compete? But anyway, when your mother was out all day sitting for the famous Mr Opie, you were allowed to dine with Mr Godwin, and your mother had said to him that he should have his meat in peace, and you were to be brought up with the pudding. You remember that he sat you on a cushion that you might reach his table, and the cushion was blue with tassels at each of its corners, and Mr Godwin and Fannikins had a sponge pudding with currants and peel, which was very fine, and he asked you about your day and how you had passed your time. And though your mother had said he should not, he put butter on your pudding.

Slow Progress

The Aunts are again in London, complaining of a 'perfectly dreadful' crossing from Dublin. Aunt Eliza, so put out by the journey, is indisposed, but Aunt Everina, who prides herself on – among other things – her cast-iron constitution, pays a visit to Skinner Street and spends most of the afternoon closeted in the study with Godwin and chaperoned by Mr Opie's portrait of Fanny's mother.

On her way out, Everina compresses her lips into a little *moue*, not unlike a cat's arsehole, and says to Fanny, 'Well, my dear, you do bear some resemblance to your mother, around the mouth at least.'

Over Everina's shoulder, Godwin makes the sign to keep it shut and Fanny smiles, with her mouth at least, and she drops a curtsy to her Aunt.

'Is my future completely decided?' Fanny asks later.

'You are a work in progress,' says Godwin.

Earache
Skinner Street, Holborn

Mrs Godwin still has a good many of her own teeth. She prizes her teeth and is zealous in the use of toothpicks and tooth powders, but despite the powders, and perhaps because of the east wind – or perhaps not – today she has a toothache, and she is not one to suffer in silence. Or alone. 'Well, of course your sisters didn't ask you to go with them, gadding about abroad again,' she says to Fanny. 'Why would they?'

Why indeed? Mr Godwin suggests a dentist, then firmly closes the door of his study, but dentists, Mrs Godwin explains to Fanny, while holding her hand to her jaw, will persist in peddling tales of toothworms, which they purport to eradicate by drilling holes into teeth and displaying nail parings or small threads and asserting that they are the corpses of the worms they have exterminated, and that will be half a crown please, plus another half a crown to stop up the hole they have made, and sixpence for something to rub on the gums. Mrs Godwin, whose pain is not so severe that she cannot speak, will have none of it, will have no truck with these so-called dental surgeons. And having declared Etherington's Tooth Tincture to be also quite useless, she must send Fanny out for laudanum to ease the pain, and laudanum can be got in many places in Holborn, it being widely used, and for many purposes, but she instructs Fanny to go directly to the apothecary on Lamb's Conduit, where they sell a reliably strong version, not the moonshine hawked for quietening infants or the settling of stomach upsets. She had thought there was still a half-bottle on the top shelf in the pantry, but it seems Mr Godwin has taken it to help him sleep when worry keeps him awake, or perhaps as a cough suppressant. No matter, Fanny must fetch more, and she is to insist that it is 'on account', which Mr Godwin will settle 'in due course'.

Fanny puts on her coat and closes the door quietly behind her.

Another Stay

Stay (noun 2a): A stationary condition, advancing neither forward nor back, a stop, a pause.
>Your whole life has felt like a stationary condition. While your sisters travelled, visited, went to school, or to the coast for their health, you stayed put in Skinner Street. Someone must mind the shop; someone must stay and be company for Godwin. You are adept at seeing he is not disturbed.

Stay (noun 2b): A temporary residence, period, or duration of such.
>After you were sent to Pentredevy, which was, after all, only a short stay **(noun 2b)**, you stay put in Skinner Street, where you are needed, a thing that supports **(noun 1a)**.

Stay (verb 2a): to cease going forward, to halt, linger, desist.

Your sisters, Mary and Claire, don't halt, linger or desist. They don't stay where they are supposed to. They have run off abroad, again:

i. To escape their scandal.

ii. Because it is cheaper to live abroad.

iii. They are appalled by the political situation in England.

iv. To get away from Godwin's constant carping about money.

v. For Shelley's health.

vi. In pursuit of Byron.

(Just take your pick, any or all of the above)

You are left behind, again. You stay at home. You stay.

Envy
Turnagain Lane, Holborn

Along Turnagain Lane, the blind man taps his way to the corner. Mrs Godwin declares it to be a ruse; he is a fraudster and sees as well as anyone else. When Fanny sees him in his usual spot, she smiles at him and he doesn't smile back. He clears his throat, spits a gob of green phlegm precisely into the gutter and begins to sing. All the while, he listens for the chink of pennies and ha'pennies falling into the hat at his feet.

Fanny has seen other blind beggars, some with open eyes, some that look like they are staring at her, some with milky, opalescent, unseeing eyes. This man's eyes are shut. No wonder he doesn't smile back. Blind or not, he doesn't even look at her. She's not worth looking at. Not even a blind beggar considers Fanny to be a catch. No one looks. No one looks twice.

She doesn't have Mary's pale brightness, Claire's creamy opulence.

In purgatory, or at least in purgatory as imagined by Dante Alighieri, the punishment for the sin of envy is to have your eyes sewn shut with wire, then labour under a coat of lead. Fanny feels its weight.

The blind man's song is a mournful one, she thinks; the words are foreign, the tune is *larghetto* or *adagio*, Claire would know which. Fanny recalls only the Welsh for slow: *araf*.

She feels awkward stopping to listen when she can't afford to pay. Can he hear her loitering?

The Dark Summer[11]
Skinner Street, Holborn

It has rained every day for a month. The shopkeepers on Snow Hill joke about building an ark. But no one laughs. Each dawn is a dark grey blanket of low cloud pressing down. They say that out in the country the corn will not ripen, Kentish hops hang limp, apples and pears fester on the branches of trees. At Skinner Street there is a worrying odour of mildew in the bookshop. Fires are lit most days, laundry refuses to dry, mould spores speckle day-old loaves. Garden paths are lush with moss. Fledglings fall out of nests. Fanny finds them, purple, blind and goggle-eyed.

At the bottom of the garden next to the bench, the one where once she sat with Shelley, is an old terracotta pot of strawberries. The plants are a riot of runners and leaves

---

***11 Dark Summer:** In 1815, in the Dutch East Indies (now Indonesia), the volcano Mount Tambora erupted, shooting large quantities of dust into the atmosphere which drifted over Europe and lingered for many months, blocking out the sunlight. Coinciding with a period of Dalton Minimum (low solar activity), 1816 was cold and wet. The poor summer was one of failed harvests, widespread food shortages, hunger, rioting, spoiled holidays and ghost stories.*

the size of hands. Still beaded from this morning's showers, those leaves promise much and deliver almost nothing. Fanny searches behind and below them for fruit. But beneath the umbrellas of those profligate leaves the fruits are scarce and mostly sour. Few gain enough sun to ripen even one side, and when they do, they lie on the wet earth to rot or to be grazed by slugs. See their slime trails? Silvery journals of their meandering.

No one has bothered to lay straw around the plants this year – the household is all at sixes and sevens, a single promissory note from financial ruin. The air is dense and tense, Fanny is worn through with it all; her head aches and her heart is sore. She misses her sisters. How many summers had they bickered over the fruit? Handkerchiefs full of berries, rich and ripe, lips stained with juice, laughing as they crammed them fast and greedy into their pretty mouths, teasing, careless girls that they were. This summer, nothing is right. The few strawberries are all for Fanny, but they are small, heart-shaped and dense with seeds.

Mary Writes
Skinner Street, Holborn

Mary writes to Fanny. Fanny's heart cavorts at the sight of her sister's hand, she swims towards the light, her lungs fill, and her mood is instantly lightened to know she was in the thoughts of the one she loves. Loves like a mother, like a lover, her skin and blister.

The letter is extravagantly several pages long and the prose well honed. It is full of description, of the journey through France and into Switzerland, the people they have encountered, their dress, their customs, the weather, the state of the roads, the sweep of the landscape – the things one might write if one was intending to publish the letter, say as part of a travelogue. A pleasant, informative letter. And cold.

But then this:

P.S. We have quite by chance encountered Lord Byron; he and Shelley are now very thick.

P.P.S. It appears that Claire was somehow – heaven knows how – already acquainted with Lord Byron! (obviously <u>do not mention this</u> to Mrs G, who would have kittens, I am sure).

Fanny Reads
Skinner Street, Holborn

Looking for ways to stay connected, to be part of Mary and Claire's world, Fanny reads the works of Byron, the more famous, more scandalous, more widely published and better-heeled poet. She reads *Childe Harold's Pilgrimage*, she reads 'The Giaour', she reads *Lara* and *The Corsair*. Her glacier of resentment begins to melt. She declares him to be a Poet. She finds she has an appetite for his work. She wonders if this time the superior quality of the poetry is also to be found in the man. She writes back: *Tell me more.*

Back Again
Skinner Street, Holborn

Then, just as suddenly as they left, they are back. And different.

Fanny longs to see her sisters. Her sisters are busy. Busy looking for a place to live in Bath. Why Bath? you might wonder. But Bath is a place where people come and go, where people don't ask too many questions. Bath is a place where Claire and Mary can gestate, one a daughter, the other a monster. Fanny has never been to Bath; she has heard it's expensive.

Shelley comes to London, but he comes alone and he comes on business – and what business is there but the money kind? He finds time to call at the shop while Godwin is out. He brings a package addressed to Fanny, and when she opens it she cries a little. Shelley looks away. 'Mary chose it,' he mumbles.

The watch is a pretty little thing, a too little too late little thing, a hasty token of the very thing that Mary will not give. Fanny puts it in her purse, in a box, away in a drawer, in a bag, in her pocket. She cannot justify keeping such a trinket; it must be worth a packet. She walks to Mr Davison's the pawnbrokers and walks home again with the watch still ticking in her pocket, with something explosive now ticking in her heart.

You tell yourself, says Fanny, that all the things you do, you do for love. Love of a sister, a mother, a minute more, but you are a liar and you would do anything to escape a future so small you wonder how you will ever squeeze yourself into it.

(Re)Animation
Churchgate, Bath

Shelley says it started with frogs, but as you might expect, it was men who took the credit: Luigi Galvani and Alessandro Volta, at the height of a thunderstorm, suspending hapless amphibians and parts of amphibians from wires. The two gentlemen, hair whipped in tendrils across their wet faces, coats darkened, flapping heavy about their ankles, wind snatching their voices. Then thunder. RUMBLE and CRACK, obliterating all other sound, and Galvani or maybe Volta counting, under his breath, counting towards the flash that will fork the sky in two.

Did they ever meet? In person, not in the intellectual space of debate between men of science which transcends the limits of our temporal and geographic planes. Did they collaborate? Was there a storm, or is that apocryphal? Does it matter that the rumble comes before the fork? Sound travels fast, light travels faster.

Shelley is drunk, slurring, sleepy, glass tilting precariously, wine will spill and stain his britches.

Galvani boasts that he has caused the frog to live (again),

Volta says no, my friend, the power, the life force, was always in and of the frog. What you have done is harnessed his spark. You have, in fact, made a battery. Volta humours Galvani by giving his name to galvanism: the puppeteering of dead things. And Volta takes credit for the battery which he can demonstrate time and again with a frog or a lemon, indoors, in the dry, and his name will signify not the thing but the power.

Now Mary has invented a story, she scribbles, feverishly.

A Further Stay

Stay (verb 2d): Be present or dwell in a place for a (specified) period; reside with a person as a guest. Dwell or reside on a regular or permanent basis.

> Or go? If the specified period of your allotted time with the Godwins is now up, you might, if they would have you, go to the Aunts Eliza and Everina in Dublin. Go to a life of chalk dust, times tables, Latin declensions, stewed tea, baskets of mending, deference. It would be a life. Of sorts.

Stay (verb 2e): Remain inactive or quiet; wait without taking action or making progress; hesitate. Delay in (doing something), defer action (until).

> Until what?

On Newton's Principles of Inertia
Gray's Inn, London

Aunt Eliza and Aunt Everina have been to London for the second time this twelvemonth. They have dined at Skinner Street several times, and in a circuitous way they have discussed their workload and their fatigue, their school and its reputation – a reputation which hangs in the balance – and how they cannot afford the disgrace of family connections with scandalous poets and the silly girls who run about after them. They have not said they will not take Fanny, but they have not finalised arrangements, they have not said when. For now, she must stay put.

Still trying to raise money for Godwin, Shelley comes to London again to see his lawyer Longdill, who according to Shelley is a weasel of a man, and he mimics Longdill and laughs at his mimicry as if it is the best of jokes. But Fanny wishes he would take serious matters more seriously.

In the afternoon, Shelley and Fanny stroll along the tree-lined walks of Gray's Inn Gardens. Without actually looking, Fanny tries to spot the footpads and pickpockets said to be

149

at work there. Without actually asking, Fanny attempts to steer their conversation so that Shelley will ask her to go to him and Mary and Claire in Bath, to visit, to stay (oh, please, to stay). But Shelley is not listening. Instead, he talks of physics. He tells her he has been reading Pemberton's work on Sir Isaac Newton, and fully expecting that she will be interested in what he has to say, he explicates some preliminary thoughts, as yet wreathing through him like smoke, about the beauty of stillness and the strength it possesses. He quotes. Fanny listens, and afterwards remembers only imperfectly.

[T]his quality in bodies, whereby they preserve their present state ... and matter, sluggish and unattractive of itself ... cannot be made to cease from inaction ... but by the opposition of a great power.

And Fanny knows herself to be matter.

Chiaroscuro
College Road, Dulwich

The man at the narrow door admits Fanny and smiles a cold, bored smile. Poor man, she thinks, he waits to go home to his dinner. The gallery, not yet open to the public, is open to students of the Royal Academy and without charge to others who apply, else Fanny would not have gone. With things at home as they are, even sixpence might not be spent freely.

She steps inside, into a cool dry hall of slanting lights and Palladian proportions, and finds to her surprise that the inside is far bigger than the outside. She gazes up at the coffered walls and domed glass ceilings. Arms wide, she turns a pirouette, her skirt flaring out, her neck stretched upwards, mouth open as if waiting for a piece of fruit delivered by a passing bird.

Down the spine of empty halls her soft shoes pat-pat-pat and she glances at the portraits of the worthy dead, the generals, the landed gentry, their wives and daughters, the philanthropists and clerics, the vain, the venerated, the men with money whose donations have made all this possible.

She lingers at pictures with a story to tell. St Paul preaching, St Sebastian enduring, Judith triumphant with the head of Holofernes. She admires the Guercino, Guido Reni, Gellée, most of all the Murillo. Gazes at a painting of the Three Graces dancing barefoot in a glade and, suppressing a smile, thinks of her mother and her Aunts – Mary, Everina, three sisters. Had they ever danced like that, girlishly, with ribbons in their hands? The two younger ones are looking up to Mary, expecting her to save them from ... from what, exactly? From themselves?

Fanny checks the time on her gold watch, the one she thinks she should probably sell but won't. It is three thirty, and the gallery will not close for another half hour. She has time. She steps on, through the halls where the pat-pat-pat of her light tread is amplified by the vastness of the rooms. The afternoon sun streams down from the skylights. The floor is patterned by alternating bands of shade. Pat-pat-pat. She reaches a door, turns the handle, but finds it locked. Pat-pat-pat, she retraces her steps, past the shipwreck, the descent from the cross, the bucolic cows drinking at a lazy river.

Disorientated now, she passes through an arch and another arch and finds herself facing a small, dark painting. Fanny feels snared by this picture; it has caught her off guard and demands she look. Objectively, she admires the composition, the light, the handling of the drapery, the subtlety of the colours – Venetian reds and umbers. A painting of three women, but these three are not dancing. One spins, one measures, one cuts. And they are old. Older than Aunt Eliza and Aunt Everina, older than all the pious dead of the portraits, older than the Bible even. These three are the Fates, Clotho, Lachesis and Atropos busily making, allotting and terminating lives. The first sister glares out towards the viewer, the second looks distractedly over her shoulder at something beyond the frame. The third sister's face is half-hidden in shadow.

Mistaken
Blackfriars Bridge

On one of the days on which she has nothing better to do – that is not to say nothing at all, for there is always a basket of mending, letters to copy for Godwin and bookshop shelves to dust, but Mrs Godwin is being particularly sharp-tongued and impossible to please – Fanny slips out of the house on some pretext or other and walks along the river embankment, where the tide is out and great shoulders of mud are exposed, glimmering slick and oily in the weak sunlight, and by the bridge at Blackfriars she thinks at first she sees the stump of a post sticking up out of the mud like a broken tooth in a leviathan jaw, but then, as she gets closer, with every step she comes to the realisation that she was mistaken and what stands there, completely motionless, is a heron, standing on one leg, looking unkempt but intense and predatory, and in spite of her melancholy mood she laughs out loud, for the heron so reminds her of Shelley, and as she laughs, tears stream down her face and she wishes with all her heart that she and her sisters had never met him and become dazzled and divided by his chaos, and as she weeps the grey heron rises silently, stiffly, long legs trailing behind like an afterthought, flaps twice as if to move on, then settles back down.

The Letter of Two Halves
Skinner Street, Holborn

Godwin has his nose in a book, in his papers, out of joint. He snaps at Mrs Godwin, and she fixes him with a steady eye and reminds him that it is her name over the door of his shop and that his financial problems are her financial problems and that he had best collect himself and write again to Mr Shelley for the money he promised, before they both end in a debtors' prison.

'And then what would become of poor Fanny?' she asks.

'Never mind Fanny. Don't bother me with Fanny. Why does Shelley now choose to live in Bath? He needs to be here in London to resolve matters and make good on his pledge to raise money.'

'A letter will reach him as easily in Bath as anywhere else.'

Godwin's note to Shelley is terse and takes only half a page. Fanny might use the remainder to write to her sister. What can be said in half a page that will bring them close again? What can be said to put right a misunderstanding and the malicious meddling of gossip that travels the route from

London to Bath and back again as freely as the post?

What Mrs Godwin said, it cannot be true. What she said that Fanny had said is certainly not true. What Mrs Godwin said that she had heard that Mary said, well, she must be mistaken. There must be a mistake; Mary would not have said that. Would she?

Rejection
Churchgate, Bath

Mary believes she is to be a writer. Every day, Mary writes. Mary is writing a story about what it's like to be rejected. Claire is bored by this new Mary and interrupts, frequently.

'We could go for a walk,' she says.

'Has the post been yet?' she asks.

Then she says: 'I do not believe that business, you know? About that thing that you heard was being said about us. Even though the part about Mama pursuing us like a hound after foxes — colourfully put — is broadly right, though she is not so lean as a foxhound. But I do not see that that, nor the other information, could have come from Fanny. Fanny would not say that about you. Tittle-tattle is certainly not her way. She has not so vulgar a soul, in fact. Fanny has the least vulgar soul of anyone I know.'

'Shut up, Claire,' say Mary.

Claire knows what it is like to be unwanted. Claire was banished to Lynmouth. Alone. Now, although she has been allowed back into Mary's golden ambit, now she is spurned by the other poet, the well-heeled, widely published, completely heartless one, the one who, although he is aware of her condition, no longer replies to the almost-daily letters she scrawls and fires off, the one who calls *her* weird. Claire is a pendulum. She loves him. He is a monster. She cannot live without him. Like the creature that Mary writes about, Claire knows what it's like to be rejected. Claire thinks Mary's story is about her.

Preparation for Flight
River Fleet

Long after Boudicca, some little time before Bazalgette, the river flows through fallow fields and on towards the bustle and stink of the city. In the early mornings, you walk the banks. Head down, a measured stride, skirts hemmed in mud, you pace the margins of this river that Pope has called a disemboguing stream. He says it is laden with dead dogs. You don't see any dogs, but the water slinks along at your side, full and brown like a mongrel bitch in pup, as she makes her way to Blackfriars to be swallowed by Old Father Thames.

The further you go, the more uneven the embankment path becomes. Where it is rutted and overgrown, you stumble. Your ankle turns awkwardly; the discomfort must be endured. You slow your pace. Breathe in the dankness. Look around at the wild fennel, hogweed, teasels, their seed heads already depleted. October is a month of dying.

In the sky, geese gather, rehearsing for their autumn exodus. Skeins forming, wings beating, muscles strengthening, each day flying a little further. This year's goslings honking anxiously in the slipstream of the older birds, birds who know where they are going, who know the stamina that will be needed. Their momentum is building. Soon they will be off.

You feel it too, the days shortening, tempers fraying, a restlessness. Debts mounting, fear of bailiffs, the summons, the knock on the door. After so long eking out a life on money that must be paid back, now it is time that is borrowed. You feel it in your skin and bone, it creeps into your marrow. You see it in the full brown slink of the water, hear it in the honk of the geese, their anticipation. You feel it just before daybreak, and you rise and walk. Each day a little further.

The Letter with the Cheque Enclosed
Skinner Street, Holborn

Godwin despises fiction. Like his wife's cats, it is a lazy indulgence and insufficiently rigorous, but unlike the cats, it may pay the rent. Fiction sells better than political philosophy, so he is writing a novel, a novel of ideas thinly disguised in a plot of drama and romance. Fanny, convinced of the merit of *Mandeville*, quietly enthuses, rubs his back where the vertebrae have begun to grind, brings him sweet tea and biscuits, weaves around him a cocoon of white lies to see he is undisturbed. She tiptoes about, like in the old days.

Godwin's publisher offered three hundred pounds, a generous advance. It had seemed like enough, but now it is all but gone. The situation goes from bad to worse. A man called Kingdon has bought a promissory note for two hundred pounds and requires immediate payment. Tradesmen call for their accounts to be settled. They call at the house and the shop. They call with increasing frequency and decreasing patience. 'Paying the rent', previously a mere figure of speech, becomes an actual problem as a landlord materialises, claims ownership of Skinner Street and makes demands about arrears. Friends are not answering letters. A further creditor, the mild-mannered Mr Blythe, regrets he has no option but to issue notice of foreclosure.

Mandeville will save the day. Will it? It must. But it is nowhere near finished. Mrs Godwin cannot for the life of her imagine why progress is so slow. Mr Godwin, shut up in his study day after day. Does he twiddle his thumbs?

The situation has an edge like a paring knife. Each day could be the one that the bailiffs come and invite Godwin to their sponging house. Each knock on the door causes hearts to stop. Blame is flung; cats skulk under the sideboard.

Fanny tries to live on air.

Shelley must make good on his proposition, offer, assurance, guarantee, promise. He has spoken of three hundred pounds. Shelley actually only has two hundred and forty-eight pounds, along with debts and pressing needs of his own. He sends two hundred.

Doors slam; curse words fly.

And worse: Shelley has made out the cheque to *William Godwin*. Godwin is outraged.

Fanny is perplexed.

Godwin and Mrs Godwin both shout and slam doors. Mrs Godwin is a nest of vipers. Godwin weighs liberty and reputation and decides a further delay must be endured. He returns the cheque with an instruction (indeed, *an instruction*) for a replacement cheque to be issued and sent forthwith, made out to a third party for cash – for how can he be expected to accept funds directly and in his own name from the philandering scoundrel who usurped his hospitality and ran off with his daughters?

Only two of his daughters, Fanny thinks.

Fanny Imlay Travels to Bath

One day, chilly, autumnal, she packs a small valise and leaves Skinner Street without a word, without anyone noticing. Her family will say afterwards that she was a good girl, biddable, unshowy, pity about the smallpox scars. If she had a fault, it was an inclination towards indolence, according to the stepfather who depended on her.

Although her earliest memories are of Scandinavia, Fanny is not used to travelling beyond London. She catches the coach to Bath, not the fast mail coach but the cheaper, regular coach, a journey of nineteen hours rumbling through the night, change at Bristol, arriving at breakfast time in the fashionable spa town where her sisters are living. Inexplicably living. Throughout the journey she rehearses her argument, sleeps a little, wakes, stares out into the blackness and starts again, building and rebuilding the castles of words in her head, searching for a way to make her case, to petition for their help. To stop the sky from falling. To ask in a way that ink cannot.

The other coach passengers will hardly remember her.

She is unremarkable. Quiet, plain-looking. Her skirt is striped, blue and white, with a small tear near the hem. Mary, who only ever did one really rash thing in her whole life, would have been more careful. Claire would have made a neater fist of the stitching.

The Undocumented Meeting
Corn Street, Bath

'A lady to see you, Miss,' says the landlord of the Bush Tavern. 'I have showed her into the front parlour.'

'Alone?' asks Fanny, but he has gone. He moves fast for a fat man. She makes her way through the public bar, crowded with travellers waiting for a change of horses, and finds Mary standing in the small private room. Standing with her back to the door, picking at something on her glove. Alone. Pity. Shelley would be more sentimental, more idealistic, more malleable. Mary is brittle. Mary still blames Fanny for the gossip that circulates about her and Shelley and Claire. Fanny has said no such thing, but Mary has called Fanny 'sordid'; Fanny is still stung. Stung, but still she craves the wasp.

'Mary,' says Fanny. 'You got my note. I would have come to you, I had asked directions—'

'Foolish,' snaps Mary. 'I mean—' She presses her lips together and Fanny catches a fleeting likeness of Aunt Everina. 'What I mean is,' she says more quietly, 'we have hardly the room to entertain.'

'Entertain?'

Fanny is not to know, but Mary is thinking that with Claire's belly expanding there is hardly room to breathe, let alone entertain. That she already has one sister too many, and why should she entertain another sister, who comes uninvited with her long face and her dismal news of Skinner Street. Comes with a straight face, expecting handouts for hypocrites when Shelley has already sent a cheque, sent as much as he could. And she comes to save face with her excuses of how she wasn't the one to pass on gossip. Gossip about Shelley's marriage and his living arrangements, and heaven knows how people will speculate now about the father of Claire's baby, a father whose identity is not to be owned, or at least not publicly owned. And here comes stupid Fanny, with her pockmarked face, smiling, meddling.

'Your papa sends—'

'Sends you to do his begging, no doubt.'

Fanny bites her lip. 'Is Shelley not with you?'

'He's not well.'

'Oh! Whatever is the matter, is it serious?'

Mary shrugs as if it were not important, but then sensing Fanny's disquiet she says that Shelley has a cough, nothing more, but he has not been sleeping and Dr Lawrence has been in attendance.

'Dr Lawrence the materialist? Not Dr Abernethy?'

'Yes, that Dr Lawrence. He is very personable, and Shelley approves now of his modern ideas. But look here, Fanny, I haven't much time to spare. What is it you would say that could not be put in a letter?'

Fanny is elsewhere. She is walking over Putney Bridge, heading for the Botanical Gardens. Walking arm in arm with her sisters, all three of them together, and discussing the spat between Dr Lawrence and Dr Abernethy, and talking about the newt, the one they kept for a pet, and strangely, the newt looks her straight in the eye and says, Of course I have a soul, why would you imagine otherwise? And it holds out one of its forelegs and Claire takes its pulse, and nods, though that only proves a heart and a circulatory system, and the newt is still looking at Fanny and looking pleased with itself. Do *you* have a soul? the newt asks her. Do you?

'Fanny.'

And the newt takes your arm in his short one, which is actually a leg, and you notice his four toes splayed out against the sleeve of your coat, and the newt does this quite conspiratorially, as if there is an understanding between you, and together you look over the parapet of the bridge. And I can swim, the newt says.

'Fanny!'

You are confused, as if you had just woken with a jolt from a brief, unplanned sleep, like waking again and again in the cramped confines of the coach as it lurched in and out of the ruts and potholes, and you reach out to steady yourself against the door frame.

You look at Mary, who is looking at you as if you have two heads, and you search for the words, words that you rehearsed through the night, but now the words are all of a jumble, jammed together as if they were stuck in the neck of a bottle, but at last they come in a rush, up your throat, but you don't ask for the desperately needed replacement for the £200 cheque that Mr Godwin sent back days ago, a foolish thing to do to be sure, but he has his pride – although you are well aware that pride is a commodity that can hardly now be afforded – and instead you say exactly what you have been wanting to say for a while now, you say, 'I want to live— that is, to come to Bath, to live with you, and we can be all together, we three, sisters like we used to be, like we should be, and I promise I will be hardly any oncost, and I can help you with the house, run errands and perhaps—'

'No,' says Mary. 'No.'

Jump, says the newt.

A Final Stay

Stay (noun 2c): A cause of stoppage, a blockage, an obstacle, a hindrance.

You are stopped, stayed, your progress halted, and paradoxically, you are also the cause of the stoppage. You are a hindrance.

In spite of your best endeavours to be no bother to anyone, you are a blockage. You cannot have tried hard enough. You have failed, and now you are stuck. You can neither stay here nor go back.

You resolve to remove the obstacle, the hindrance. You will go to a place where you are not known, somewhere you cannot be stopped. Maybe, if money were no object, if nothing got in your way, you could keep on heading west until you reached the edge of the map, maybe you could fall off the end of the earth. Maybe if you sell the little gold watch, you could go that far. Or maybe Swansea will be far enough?

Apothecary
Corn Street, Bath

They say there's a shop on Corn Street, not too far, not difficult to find. You walk past a couple of times, but you are resolved. The sign over the door says HASSALL & WILLIAMS. A narrow sort of place. You slide in. It has a dry, woody smell with undertones of mace and perhaps something bitter. You take off your gloves. The fussy little man who bustles from a room at the back looks exactly as an apothecary should look, small and bald with wire-framed spectacles and a cadaverous complexion.

'Sydenham's is excellent,' he says. 'I recommend Sydenham's Laudanum to all my lady clients. Two drops in water or in a small glass of wine will guarantee a good night's sleep. A little more perhaps for, ah, relief, pain relief.'

You scan the densely packed shelves: a place for everything, and everything in its place. Everything sorted and slotted into its pigeonhole. Holes where pigeons might roost; you imagine birds, nestled, feathered, warm and settled, a complacent cooing, the smell of dust and husks.

'Yes?' he prompts.

'Yes.'

He fetches a bottle from a high shelf and wraps it in brown paper. You hand over the money, you take the bottle, a little ribbed-glass escape hatch, and slide it into your bag.

'When you want some more, come and see me. I'm open six days a week.'

'Oh, no, I won't be ... well, of course. Thank you.'

No, of course you won't. This is the last time, for sure. And you are sure. You bow and back out of the little shop into the street with passers-by scurrying, a dog tied in a doorway shivering, fine rain drizzling, starlings murmuring.

The Fall

You remember when you were Fannikins. You remember a teacup. A pattern around its rim of birds in blue and white. You pretended being already grown-up and allowed to sip from the cup and it seemed to you, in that moment, that time thickened, lush and silky as the damask tablecloth pleated in the fingers of your other hand. But when you tried to place the fine cup back on its saucer, time was as thin as air and the teacup sailed away from you and was already on the floor, exploded into a thousand shards that sprang out like sparks, and Mama shrieked.

You knew she must be angry; she had said do not touch. Tears welled in your eyes, tears of fright and shame, but she gathered you in to her, folded you in her arms, and kissed your fingers until the blood was quite kissed away. And she smelt of tea leaves and ink.

The Crossing from New Passage
Severn Estuary and Churchgate, Bath

Travelling for days, increasingly devoid of any sense of direction. Not entirely sure how far you will go, only that it no longer matters. First, the overnight coach from London to Bristol, then from Bristol to Bath and back to Bristol again same day, a bad day. Very bad. You shouldn't have gone to Bath, should have known they wouldn't want you. Mary wouldn't want you. Of course she doesn't want you. An overnight stay in Bristol, not bothering to eat, letters to write, a sleepless night, eyes red and swollen till you were all cried out. This morning's transport is more rustic, a cart to the ferry at New Passage, your hips squashed between the rough-sawn sides and the soiled trousers of a man whose cockerel shits on the luggage piled at the back. At least you have no luggage.

Once out of the town, the land becomes flat and drab, and as you near the river the wind ruffles your hair, lifts your coat, chaps your lips. It carries a barely perceptible spray of rain, the tang of salt water and mudbanks. You arrive crumpled and bone-sore. A bleak sort of place, there's an inn, but you don't go inside. You sit on a bench, leeward of the wind. You sit with your buttoned boots neatly together; your hands folded in your lap. You sit alone, feeling empty, feeling numb. The ferry is due in just under an hour and you watch for it as it inches its way across the estuary, labouring against the suck and pull of the ebb tide.

Eventually, the ferry heaves to, muddy water swirls, men haul rope, make fast, and a mule is coaxed to walk backwards behind her cart, ready to receive freight. Green-gilled passengers eye the jetty, waiting for their turn to disembark. The crossing has been a rough one, they say.

'Mind your step, miss,' says the ferryman as he hands you aboard.

'Fanny was absolutely impossible yesterday,' complains Mary to Claire. 'You know how she gets, all *poor me* and *none of this is my fault*. Saying she wants us all to be together again, to be close again. But she can't come here.'

'Well, she'll find out anyway, in the end,' says Claire, spreading her hands across her belly. 'They all will. I don't see that it matters.'

'Oh, you're such a child. Of course it matters. Besides, there is Godwin to think of — who else would look after him? And then there's Shelley. And your reputation.'

They sit on their acid-yellow velveteen sofa in fashionable Bath, they drink tea, they read, send letters, they walk a little, they wait for Shelley to return. And though they have lived so much in the past two years, they are both little more than children, playing house.

'You know if the tables were turned, and you went knocking on Fanny's door, she'd take you in. She'd take you in in a heart-beat,' says Claire to Mary.

Through a spatter of drizzle, you watch the ropes strain, the water slap against the hull. Horses, blindfolded, led over planks and onto the ferry. Sacks and crates stacked aboard. You must wait for the turn of the tide.

Mary scowls because she knows it's true; Fanny's love is like a blanket. But she is so sick of sisters, sick of the one she is stuck with, sick of the other, who would suffocate her with her love.

The ferry pulls away from the shore; you feel a lurch as the banks slurp, the current pulls one way, the wind another, sails fill, rudder creaks, the helmsman turns his back on England, steers for the Black Rock and the mouth of Wales.

Claire yawns; she finds pregnancy exhausting. Mary smooths her dress and says, to herself, mostly to herself, mostly *for* herself, 'Impossible, you know how she gets. Whatever else was I supposed to do?' and tucks her hair neatly behind her ears.

You grip the side rail and stare down into the heave and surge, the mud soup of the estuary mixing with the swirl of the incoming tide. You think of your mother; you hold her hand as she prepares to jump from Putney Bridge. What must it be like, you wonder, to tumble headlong into the water, to cartwheel over and over, your skirts billowing out, filling and refilling? Your hair unspooling like seaweed, your mouth, your eyes, your ears full of water.

'Fanny will get over it. By the time she's back home in Skinner Street, she will have come to her senses,' says Mary.
'Ah, poor old Fan,' says Claire. 'Perhaps we might write to her?'

But you have written first, advising them of your departure.

Laudanum
Mackworth Arms, Wind Street, Swansea

The little bottle stayed in your bag while you wrote, while you tried to sleep, while you travelled west, on the cart, on the ferry, on foot. Now, you are alone and you have turned the key in the lock of the door of the plainly furnished room. No one knows you here, and you won't be disturbed. Now you take the bottle from your bag, unwrap it, and being of a frugal disposition, you smooth out the brown paper in case it might be of some use, then place the bottle on the side table next to the bed.

Walk up and down, up and down; the last time you will walk anywhere.

Everything is as it should be. The letters you wrote will have been delivered. You think you have made yourself clear, though it is hardly an easy matter to explain – not even to yourself – even though you are sure. And you *are* sure. There has been no cataclysm, just a series of doors closing. You are tired of trying to be small enough not to be any bother. There is no point in being more than the narrow slot of your future, or more than other hearts can accommodate. And love, of course, it has always been about love. You have tried to tell them that. But anyway, that is all done with. It is time to go. They will make of it what they will. And *they* are done with. There is only you. You drink your tea. The teacup is blue and white, a pattern of birds flying around the rim. And you are sure.

Unstopper the bottle and sniff.

Stare out of the window onto the street. Flickers of lamplight reflect off the rain-slicked cobbles, but no one is watching. In the distance, a cat yowls in displeasure and you laugh, but quietly, and to yourself. You pause for a little time, time enough for composure, not enough for second thoughts. With only a small amount of difficulty, you manage to open the window, sliding the bottom sash up, letting in the night air.

Pour the contents of the bottle, yes, all of it, best to be sure, into your empty teacup.

A colour not dissimilar to tawny port.

Unbutton your boots, place them side by side under the table. They need reheeling, but that is of no importance now.

Sip.

Tastes of rust.

Sip.

Then a dry, woody bitterness that resolves into saffron, cloves, mace and the warm buzz of canary wine.

Drink it. Drink it all, that's it, swallow it down.

Cough, splutter, some runs out of the side of your mouth.

A dirty sediment remains in the bottom of the cup. You wonder if the sediment might be read like tea leaves, telling that narrow future that doesn't matter any more. And you think of the palmist at the fairground on the fields in Kennington and everything he predicted and what a charlatan he was.

Lie down on the bed.

Sleep now.

Arms by your side, then folded across your chest, then smooth your hair, arms repositioned, try to relax, hands folded over your stomach; smooth your skirts, flex your fingers. Useless arms don't know where to be. You wonder what will become of the little gold watch; it is in your purse, its faltering ticks muffled by a handkerchief.

Sleep now.

But sleep won't come.

You are not sure it's going to work. Have you taken enough?

Have you?

Eventually, a little drowsiness.

Heaviness. Leaden arms no longer restless. It is very much as you hoped it would be. Very much like falling asleep.

Breathing becomes shallow. And slows.

And slows.

Heart slows.

Not like the tick of the watch in need of winding, lurching from one tick to the next, but gently, a folding inward. Like folding up something to put it away in a drawer.

And then at last, although you did not choose the river, you find you *are* in the water; it is warm and silent. And your skirts are not billowing – you are very thankful for that. Everything is satisfactory. You are leaving nothing behind, or everything. You are leaving sisters. You drift. There is no urgency; time is of no moment here. And you drift, and the broad and unhurried river wraps around you, taking care of you, guiding you, and although you never learnt to swim, you know what to do. You feel in your pockets for the smooth, round pebbles of memories, and you take them out, and you let them go. They sink and disappear, and as they are enveloped by the dark velvet mud of the riverbed, you kick, and rise, upwards, up towards the surface, towards the light.

Stays

Stay (noun 3. Always plural: stays, *a pair of stays*): A corset made of two pieces laced together and stiffened by the insertion of strips of whalebone etc., worn to shape and support (restrict, contain, control, limit and fetter).

>The next morning, when she is found dead in an upstairs room in the perfectly respectable Mackworth Arms Hotel in Swansea, the unnamed young lady is wearing a pair of stays marked for the laundry, with the initials M.W. Did Fanny even for an instant consider loosening those stays? Making herself comfortable? Or did she prefer instead to be moulded into a proper shape? Decent, modest, narrow. Or, alternatively, did she feel encircled, supported, held and embraced?

A Change of Address

> *I have long determined that the best thing I could do was to put an end to the existence of a being whose birth was unfortunate, and whose life has only been a series of pain to those persons who have hurt their health in endeavouring to promote her welfare. Perhaps to hear of my death will give you pain, but you will soon have the blessing of forgetting that such a creature ever existed as*

Written on the evening of 9 October 1816, this note was published a few days later in the Swansea newspaper, *The Cambrian*, along with an editorial comment that *the name appears to have been torn off and burnt.*

You might have noticed the change of address: '... *to hear of my death will give you pain* ...' A direct address. Not to 'those persons', but '*you*'. You?

Coda: A Curious Visitor
Via Romana, Florence, 1878

'Miz Clairmont, ma'am? Miz Clairmont? Oh, you are awake, I wasn't sure. I hope I'm not disturbing you, ma'am. It's very good of you to see me at last. Very good indeed. I have so many questions I'd like to put to you about Mr Shelley, and about your sister, such an angel. An angel! What a life! What a remarkable life! And you must surely have such memories? So many intriguing documents? A wealth of information?'

Claire peers at the gentleman from the shady comfort of her lace mantilla, an affectation, but at her age – and she's now almost eighty – who cares? He says his name is Silsbee, Edward Silsbee, from Massachusetts, and he is greatly interested in acquiring some old letters. He seems respectable enough, if perhaps a little fawning. Like a mastiff that has eaten something it shouldn't. A fawning mastiff in fawn chequered trousers, very modern, very American.

Claire sighs with no pretence at all at politeness. 'My sister,' she says at last. 'I've been thinking about her a lot lately. My sister was, after all, an extraordinary woman.'

185

'And such a romance between them? Between your sister and Mr Shelley,' the man in the chequered fawn trousers prompts.

'Well, I think she understood him. There was something between them, certainly something.'

'The romance of the century?'

'Oh, no! Not that. I think—' Claire leans forward, coughing into a handkerchief, a spasmic cough that suggests derision.

'You were saying?' he says.

'Not romance, but Romanticism. He had a deeply flawed and selfish energy. I think my sister – Fanny – I think that from the start, *she* saw Shelley for exactly what he was, as a poet and as a man. Fanny didn't mistake one for the other. She said it was from the smallest things that one learns the most of character. I realise now she must have been extraordinarily *clear-sighted*.'

'But *Mary* Shelley, ma'am, the writer of *Frankenstein*—'

'Oh, *that* sister.'

Claire closes her eyes, yawns, and feigns the sleep she waits for.

Ends and Loose Ends

1816   Fanny's body is unclaimed. The coroner declares her 'found dead', and she is buried in an unmarked grave at the expense of the parish. She is twenty-two.

In December, Harriet Westbrook (Shelley's first wife) commits suicide by drowning in the Serpentine. She is twenty-one and heavily pregnant. Mary and Shelley are married.

1817   In January, Claire gives birth to a daughter, Alba, whose name she later changes to Allegra. Byron acknowledges the child as his. He writes to a friend, This comes of *'putting it about'*.

1818   Mary's novel *Frankenstein; or, the Modern Prometheus* is published – but anonymously. She is twenty.

Mary, Shelley and Claire, along with their three young children, leave England for Italy.

Byron takes charge of Allegra. He places her with a number of different foster families and then in an Italian convent.

Mary and Shelley's daughter Clara dies of dysentery in Venice, aged one.

1819 Mary and Shelley's son William, 'Wilmouse', dies of malaria in Rome, aged three

1822 Allegra dies of typhoid fever aged five.
Shelley drowns in a boating accident during a storm off the Gulf of La Spezia, aged twenty-nine.

1824 Byron dies of a fever at Missolonghi while fighting in the Greek War of Independence, aged thirty-six.

1836 Godwin dies, aged eighty.

1841 Mrs Godwin dies, aged seventy-three (or thereabouts).

1844 Sir Timothy Shelley dies, aged ninety-one.

1851 Mary dies of a brain tumour in England, aged fifty-four. She is survived by her fourth child, Percy Florence Shelley, who has inherited his paternal grandfather's title and estate. His wife burns many of Mary's letters.

1879 Claire Clairmont (who never married) dies in Florence, aged eighty-one.

Acknowledgements:

'A Little Spark May Yet Remain' was first published in *Lighthouse 28* (Bawburgh, Norfolk, 2024).

'A Lecture on Electricity, Phantasmagoria and the Gasses' was first published in the anthology *The Weather Where You Are* (Bath, 2023).

'Preparation For Flight' was first published in the anthology *Monsoon* (Cambridge, 2025).

An early version of 'Fanny Imlay Travels to Bath' was first published as 'Fanny Imlay Travels to Swansea with a Bottle of Laudanum in Her Bag' in the anthology *Snow Crow* (Bath: Ad Hoc Fiction, 2021).

THE HYENA'S DAUGHTER

JUPITER JONES

First published in 2026
by Weatherglass Books

Copyright © 2026 Jupiter Jones

All rights reserved. No part of this publication may be reproduced or transmitted in any form or by any means, electronic or mechanical, including photocopy, recording or any information storage and retrieval system, without permission in writing from the publisher.

This book is a work of fiction. Names, characters, businesses, organizations, places and events are either the product of the author's imagination or used fictitiously. Any resemblance to actual persons, living or dead, or events is entirely coincidental.

A CIP record for this book is published by the British Library

ISBN: 978-1-0681766-0-9

Cover design: Tom Etherington
Typesetting: James Tookey

Printed in the U.K. by CMP Books, Dorset

www.weatherglassbooks.com

Weatherglass
Books